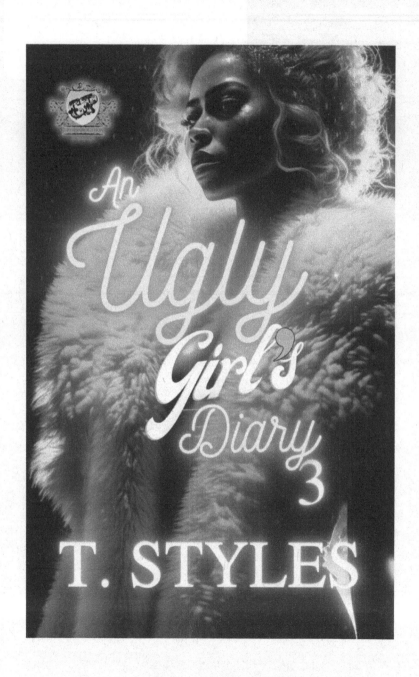

An Ugly Girl's Diary 3

T. STYLES

ARE YOU ON OUR EMAIL LIST?

SIGN UP ON OUR WEBSITE

www.thecartelpublications.com

By T. STYLES

CHECK OUT OTHER TITLES BY THE CARTEL PUBLICATIONS

AN UGLY GIRL'S DIARY 3

WWW.THECARTELPUBLICATIONS.COM

By T. STYLES

AN UGLY GIRL'S

DIARY 3

By

T. STYLES

Library of Congress Control Number: 2024901874

ISBN 10: 1948373947

ISBN 13: 978-1948373944

Cover Design: Book Slut Girl

First Edition

Printed in the United States of America

By T. STYLES

What up Fam,

What's good? As the world keeps spinning and we keep winning, I'm sliding through with that real and crazy love straight from the heart. Y'all know how we do it at Cartel Publications, always keeping it a buck!

Now, let's chop it up about the latest banger, *"An Ugly Girl's Diary 3"*. T. Styles ain't just spinning yarns, she weaving whole tapestries where every thread is a nerve. This joint gonna take you on a ride so buckle up and see if you can guess where you're going!

Now, let's shift our focus and keep in line with tradition. In this novel, we want to give love to,

LAMAR DEMEATRICE JACKSON JR.

If you're unaware, *Lamar D. Jackson Jr.* is an NFL quarterback for the Baltimore Ravens for the past five years! However, this season he has taken the team to the AFC Championship game being played in Baltimore for the first time in franchise history! In fact, by the time y'all get this book, the Ravens would have won and be on their way to the Superbowl!! (Fingers crossed) Or they lost...but I'm hoping it's a W! Either way, I'm proud of the team and I'm super proud of Lamar! He is incredible and I know he will bring many Superbowl's to the city of Bmore!

Aight...As Lamar has said all season...lock in, fam. It's time to get comfortable, kick back with your snack of choice, and let the story wash over you like the love we pour into every line. This is for the dreamers, the believers, the underdogs this one's for you!

Stay up, stay blessed, and never forget...we are the stories we tell, and this one's gonna be legendary.

One Love!

C. Wash

Vice President

The Cartel Publications

www.thecartelpublications.com

www.facebook.com/authortstyles

www.facebook.com/Publishercwash

Instagram: Publishercwash

Instagram: Authortstyles

www.twitter.com/cartelbooks

www.facebook.com/cartelpublications

By T. STYLES

www.theelitewritersacademy.com

Follow us on IG: Cartelpublications

Follow our Movies on IG: Cartelurbancinema

#CartelPublications

#UrbanFiction

#PrayForCece

#LamarJackson

#BaltimoreRavens

#ANUGLYGIRLSDIARY3

By T. STYLES

PROLOGUE
CURRENT DAY

It was a bitterly cold fucking night, as Courtney Martin shivered, not just from the chill but from the realization of where she found herself: an uninviting shack she had no business being inside in the first place.

She was completely naked.

Beside her lay her large Louis Vuitton purse, its contents haphazardly scattered on the ground. The most valuable item she had was her cell phone, which, frustratingly, had no service. Equally important was her diary, her constant companion.

Something she wrote in every day.

While her teeth chattered, she berated herself for her foolishness, for getting entangled in a game she had willingly played, yet she knew anyone in her situation would have fought tooth and nail for what they believed was rightfully theirs.

But it wasn't just any fight. It was for her life's work, her sense of security.

Her fucking money.

She refused to be robbed of it again!

Not after fighting so hard.

Surveying the shack, Courtney's eyes landed on a milk crate and an old, stiff potato sack. The cold sharpened her wits. What was she going to do? Use the sack for warmth or lay it on the crate to avoid splinters piercing her skin.

She chose to put it on the crate.

Once settled, she peered through the wooden slats in front of her. The world outside was covered in darkness, save for a distant house with a lit window. She decided to stay motionless, more frozen than ever, for this standoff of her life.

Diving back into her purse, she retrieved her diary.

Regret flickered through her heart because a knife or even the retractable bat she owned would have been more useful in this situation. Yet she knew dwelling on 'what ifs' wouldn't help. She needed a clear mind.

Maybe her diary could provide clarity.

Opening the flap to the first dated entry six months ago.

Courtney began to read...

By T. STYLES

CHAPTER ONE

May 3rd, 2023

Dear Diary,

Everybody hates me.

The amount of reaction videos to my content and the amount of angry mail I get is so heavy, that I told my team don't show me anymore.

If it wasn't for my son and my man, I would feel alone.

And even now I'm starting to think that my nigga is over me. We've been solid 'til now. But lately he feels off. After spending so much time with a person whether they say it or not, you know if something has changed.

The first time we met?

It was kind of cute.

If you keep an open mind.

Last year I was in a diner, waiting on a sponsor I was supposed to be meeting. When I went to grab a sugar jar off another table because mine was empty, he walked up to me, whispered in my ear, and said, 'You should go home.'

I'm like, 'Excuse you?' He's fine as fuck, but I don't care. Why's he even talking to me, let alone telling me to go home?

I laugh when I think about it now. Because we're so compatible.

And then he tells me, 'We got a meeting.'

I'm confused.

Since I'm very private not many recognize me from 'An Ugly Girl's Diary' podcast.

But he knew me on sight.

How?

Of course he was the one I was waiting for. It's just that he was more perfect in person. His IG pic didn't do him justice.

I sat back down in the booth. "First of all you're late. And why do you want me to go home anyway?" I poured sugar into my coffee.

He sat down, leaned in, and whispered, 'Cause you got blood on your clothes. The back of your pants.' I nearly died, Diary!

This is why I dread meetin' new people. Not 'cause of some period mishap like I had in front of Mr. Fine, but 'cause I'm socially awkward. Always the wallflower, safe in my corner, no competition.

I just...

"Bae…"

Courtney closed her diary when she heard Plazo walk in. She was wearing her robe and it showed her light brown skin, and the strawberry patch tattoo adorning her shoulder blade. Looking up at him with hazel Brown eyes, she said, "Yes? Do you want anything for breakfast?"

At 47, he was a towering presence with his dark, silky skin. His beard was a distinguished blend of black with streaks of grey, which added to his youthful face.

He sat next to her and put his hand on her leg. She loved when he did that because in her mind it meant he cared. "No, I'm just surprised you're writing in that thing so early." He pointed at it as if it were a dirty magazine.

"What you mean?"

"Don't you have to take Lawson to school?"

"Oh, fuck! And he has football practice this morning. Like they don't give us enough stuff to do as is." She looked at the time on her watch surprised she let it get away from her. But Plazo was on her mind because if that man left her at that point in her life, she would have a tough time sorting things out.

"Something is bothering me." She pushed her hair out of her face and tucked it behind her ear. "I need to know right now what you're going to do."

"What you talking about?"

"Plazo, I know things haven't been good with us–"

"I care about you. And, I'm gonna fight for us as long as I can. At the same time it's not the right time to talk about this. You got to take Lawson to school. But I'm going to be here when you get home." He leaned over and kissed her. "Trust." He squeezed her leg again and walked out the room.

She wasn't sure if he meant to do it or not but he damn sure eased her mind. At least briefly. Dropping the diary in her purse she went to see about her son.

Walking into the living room, she took a moment to observe her home and open up the house. This meant opening the blinds. She loved how the sun crept up over the roof, spilling its light inside. As if it was a spotlight, that shined love on the environment she was providing for her son. In addition to the comfortable clutter of a life lived hard.

And then there were the photos. Despite her not being in most of the pictures. Because after all this time, Courtney still had a problem with her own reflection. And there was nothing anybody could do to tell her differently.

Not even her boyfriend, Plazo.

"I know you're not trying to do homework at the last minute. Not when you know I got a meeting and have to get to my studio."

Her son, fifteen-year-old Lawson, lounged on the couch, textbooks and headphones scattered around him. His dreadlocks draped his face and blended into the beard and stash he had working.

"Ma, why you sweating me?" Lawson's voice, deepening with adolescence, broke the morning stillness. "I heard Plazo just tell you to come in here. Because you were in that diary again."

"You talking to who right now?"

"You know what I mean, ma."

"I'm not one of your friends, Lawson. You'd do well to remember it."

When she turned her head under his breath, he said "I know, but I wish you were sometimes." He looked at her as she fussed with buttoning her shirt.

As she served scrambled eggs and wheat toast, her movements were somewhat ruffled. The very important sponsor, who she preferred to talk to over the phone was probably waiting on her at her favorite diner.

Courtney glanced at the clock, time was tight as usual. But lately weird things had been happening. People left strange notes on her front porch. Sent packages with nothing in them and even called her without saying anything. So she liked to make sure the coast was clear before bringing her son outside in the morning.

When she opened the front door and peaked out, she saw a paper bag. From the smell of it, she could tell it was shit. It seemed like every other week, it was something. She started to be immune to it because sometimes it felt childish. But if her son suffered a setback, she would go off for sure.

After throwing it in the trash on the curb, and examining her car, which was fine, she went back in the house.

"Let's bounce, Lawson! Now!"

Just as disheveled as his mother, he tossed everything into his book bag and followed her outside the door.

Once in the car, and when the seatbelts clicked, she said, "Don't forget I'm picking you up."

"Ma, when you gonna let me take the bus? Or walk to school. You treat me like a kid."

She frowned. I mean had he met her ever? "You're my son. And I'm gonna treat you like that because I want you safe. Be glad you got a mother who cares."

When she parked in front of Todd Davis high school, in Washington DC, Courtney fixed his shirt and made sure his jacket was nice and neat.

"Ma, I know you want to fix everything, but sometimes it feels like you're fighting ghosts of the past instead of fighting for yourself."

"What you talking about?"

"It feels like you're pushing me in a hole over something that probably happened before I was born. I mean after all this time, ain't we safe?"

She was stunned.

For starters, it seem like he had that one in the chamber. Ready to go at the right time. She was somewhat impressed, but she also felt embarrassed.

He kissed her on the cheek and exited the car. All she could do was watch as he disappeared into the school. He was becoming a grown ass man.

Courtney slipped into the booth at the bustling local restaurant, the aroma of coffee and sizzling bacon filling the air. She spotted the sponsor, Tasha, waving from a corner table. And just the sight of the woman had her feeling inferior already.

She was beautiful, despite being much older than her. Clear skin. Fashionable clothing and a smile that said everything was good in her life. At least Courtney thought from the outside looking in.

She hadn't even met her formally yet. She hustled in her direction.

"Hey girl, you found me!" Tasha greeted her with a bright smile, the bonnet from her line dazzling in an array of colors.

Courtney waved back.

"I was afraid you wouldn't get my message in time about where I was sitting. And I decided I didn't want to sit at the breakfast counter."

"Actually I didn't get your message. But I couldn't miss that bonnet anywhere. I love how you wear it in the street. Monique would probably go off though.

You're a walking billboard, for real," Courtney laughed, settling in, fussing with her clothing in the process. Had she known she was going to be so cute, she would've dressed better.

Instead, she was too busy, throwing bags of shit in the trashcan on her curb.

Tasha chuckled, pouring them both a glass of orange juice, subtlety spiked with champagne. "Gotta represent, right? So, let's talk." Suddenly she paused while looking at Courtney a bit harder. "Are you okay? You seem out of it."

Maybe the woman was Auntie after all. I mean how did she know that the conversation she had with her son was still on her heart?

"I'm good."

Tasha nodded slowly, not fully believing her. "Okay, if you don't wanna tell me, I understand." She took a deep breath. "As I mentioned, I think your listeners would love my specialized bonnets. Because as you and I both know not all bonnets are created equally. Some of us like our short styles, some of us wear wigs and sew ins–"

"Or locs."

"Exactly. And my product allows them to keep it cute while they sleep. I mean your man probably won't like it but still."

Courtney raised her glass, "Cheers to that. I can see it now, 'Sleep Pretty with Tasha's Bee Nets'." The two clinked glasses, the light mood infectious.

"I knew you would see things my way!"

"So how many spots did you want to sponsor?" Courtney took a deep sip. Normally her engineer/business partner, Adrienne would handle all of these things. But the woman wanted to meet with her personally.

"Let's just say I'm willing to spend $20,000 over the course of six months. If it does better, I'll do more."

She almost spit out her orange juice. "That's great!"

"Although there is something else I will need. I will want to see you in the bonnet on air. I realize you only do audio and don't have a YouTube channel but—."

"I can get my engineer to wear—."

"It has to be you." Tasha was firm. Not nasty but business like. "I mean, why don't you want to show yourself? You're beautiful!"

Courtney beautiful? She was an ugly girl to hear her tell it.

Before she could respond Courtney's phone buzzed. Removing it from her Louis Vuitton purse she glanced at the screen, her expression turned to fear as she read the message from her engineer.

"Everything cool?" Tasha asked, noticing the change in Courtney's demeanor.

Courtney bit her lip, rereading the message. "It's...it's my engineer. Says there's been somebody cruising by the office. More than once."

Tasha's brows knitted in concern. "That don't sound right. You think it's related to your podcast?"

"I don't know. It's been happening for over a month. Every time she tells me I get nervous. But it could be nothing," Courtney replied, her voice tinged with worry.

Tasha, nodded, looked down and back at her. "Did you want to continue?"

"Of course."

"Look, I'm a fan of your show. That's one of the reasons why I wanted to sponsor your podcast. You do a lot for many women who have been walked over. Taken advantage of. But your podcast despite being controversial really forces women to speak up. To have a voice."

"Lately, I'm not sure if it's worth it. And then there's my home situation."

"If you don't mind me, asking, what's going on?"

"I think my man may be tired of the hours. At least that's what I'm left to believe considering he doesn't want to talk about it."

"I'm sorry to hear that. You've got a voice that's shaking things up, making people listen. But that can make you a target too," Tasha said, her tone serious. "In your personal life or your business. But anything great comes at a cost."

Courtney nodded, her mind racing. She was literally teaching women how to get back at the people who burned them.

She was talking about destroying there predators.

So of course she was a target!

For some reason, Courtney couldn't get comfortable. "Look, I wanted to sit with you a bit longer but I gotta check this out, make sure everything's straight," She grabbed her purse and slid out of the booth.

Tasha reached out, touching her arm. "Be careful, Courtney. And call me...let me know you're okay."

Courtney offered a strained smile. "Will do."

"Also remember, I need your face if we're going to make this deal. It's non-negotiable."

Courtney nodded.

As she rushed to her Benz parked outside, her mind was a whirlwind of thoughts. The city streets blurred past as she drove quickly, her hands gripping the steering wheel, the weight of her responsibility loud and clear in her heart.

To her child, her man, her listeners.

Suddenly, after all this shit, between whoever was lurking, and Tasha wanting her to step out of her comfort zone, the morning sun no longer seemed as bright.

She was preoccupied with the troubling text as she navigated the busy streets to her office. That's when she spotted her – a young lady, barely holding herself up against a light post, looking lost and drunk as fuck.

But this early?

Keeping a wide view at all times, her heart skipped a beat when she noticed three men closing in, their intentions unclear but their approach unsettling.

Without a second thought, Courtney swung her Benz to the curb, almost hitting a delivery truck in the process. He was gonna be alright. But the girl may not be if she didn't mix in. And so, her protective instincts kicked in as she approached the group, her voice firm yet calm.

"Everything okay here?" Courtney's tone was low.

What was she doing?

She wasn't this person.

Maybe her son's words hit her hard. But if she wasn't careful, it would also get her punched in the face.

The men, caught off guard, tried to brush her off. "We know her, just helping her out," one of them said, a false smile smeared on his face. His voice was so deep she wondered if it was fake.

Courtney turned to the girl, a cute young thing with braids, who looked up with dazed, fearful eyes. "You...you know them?" She asked gently.

The girl shook her head, clinging to the post. Her hand hovered over her stomach. It looked as if she were about to throw up. "No, I... I don't know them."

That was all Courtney needed to hear. "Alright, you're coming with me," she said decisively, guiding the girl away from the men and towards her car.

"Hey, where you think you taking her?" One called out, a hint of aggression in his voice. "I said we know her."

"Then what's her name?"

Silence.

"That's what I thought."

Courtney didn't flinch, helping the girl into the passenger seat quickly before things got violent. And it looked like it was going to go in that direction. Because the men were approaching the car quickly. When the girl was safe, she rushed into the driver seat and sped off.

Breathing heavily, she weaved in and out of traffic as if they could catch her on foot. She was in her own head. In her own thoughts. Her heart pounded but when she looked to the right, she saw the girl was just as afraid.

"You're safe now. What's your name?"

The girl, her words slurred, mumbled something that sounded like "Sakura."

"Alright, Sakura, I'm Courtney. I'm taking you to my office, okay? We'll get you some help there. Did you want to call the police?"

"Please don't get them involved. They don't understand people like me."

"I get it."

To be honest, she was relieved the girl said no. Courtney was already late, and now she was participating in this unexpected detour. But she couldn't just leave her alone in her state and so she didn't. Five minutes later, she pulled up to the office, helping Sakura inside.

Her staff members covered them quickly. Like Courtney was bringing home a new toy. "This is Sakura. Please get her something to eat and let her sleep on the couch in my office."

"No problem."

"Did you see the men driving around the office again?" Courtney asked.

"Could be a woman. But to answer your question, not since Adrienne called you."

Her staff quickly refocused back on Sakura. One of them, Keisha, brought her some coffee and a sandwich while Courtney worked to prepare for her show.

"What happened to her?" Keisha asked as she set the food down.

Courtney sighed, running a hand through her hair. "Long story."

Courtney strode into the studio, the air buzzing with the typical pre-show energy. Despite telling her to get some rest, for some reason, Sakura trailed behind, still shaky but in the caring hands of Courtney's staff. There was something about Courtney that she gravitated to, and she wanted to breathe in every moment.

But Adrienne wasn't so friendly. "Who is that? And why is she in here?"

"Girl, she with me. She's all right. Are you ready?"

Adrienne nodded.

Keisha guided Sakura to the sofa. "Don't say nothing or speak while they are on air."

"I got it."

When Courtney was seated, her engineer flipped the switch. The red 'On Air' sign flickered to life, and Courtney slipped into her professional persona, her voice confident and resonant as it flowed through the microphone.

She began discussing today's topic of twin sisters, who were dating twin brothers only to learn that both brothers were unfaithful. Things were compounded when it was discovered that they left both of them at the altar during a double wedding. It was going to be such a big event that even the newspaper and popular radio stations were coming.

Courtney was livid.

And in her usual smooth way gave them all the skills necessary to get revenge. I mean she had a serious ass plan. On ways to not only make sure every female, who may be interested, knew who they were dealing with, but also to impact their business, a tire shop in Baltimore.

Since they were streaming, although not visually, comments were rolling in agreeing that Courtney was the goat. That nobody knew how to set shit straight like their leader.

But twenty minutes into the show, something shifted.

The comment board, usually filled with questions, support, and occasional banter, was suddenly flooded with ominous messages. "Very soon you'll meet your fate."

The messages were back-to-back.

Drowning out the energy of fans who were showing love.

"Hold up, you see that shit!" Keisha asked Adrienne.

She nodded. "I do."

Courtney's heart pounded in her chest and she tried to maintain her composure, but her voice faltered, the words catching in her throat. She glanced through the studio glass at her team, their faces filled with concerned.

There had to be hundreds or even thousands of messages back-to-back. All saying the same thing.

"Yo, Courtney, you good?" Adrienne whispered.

She nodded as she bore witness to the messages still pouring in.

Was this a sick prank related to whoever was circling the office? A threat from someone she'd exposed on her show? Or something worse. Did someone want to take revenge out on her? Or her family?

The walls of the studio felt like they were closing in, each message a hammer strike to her already fragile sense of safety.

"Well, diary fanatics!" Adrienne interrupted. "If you like Gina's grass hotdogs, check them out now at the local grocers."

Keisha frowned. "What the fuck is that?" She whispered. "That's not a sponsor."

"Don't worry it's fine," she whispered, covering her mic. "Well fanatics, that's it for today's show. We'll be back soon!"

Her engineer wrapped up the segment hastily, her usual smooth sign-off replaced with a *fuck off* type of energy. As soon as the 'On Air' sign dimmed, Courtney ripped off her headphones and stepped out of the studio, her facade crumbling.

"Where you think these comments coming from?" Keisha demanded.

Adrienne shook her head, scrolling through the comments. "I don't know, but we need to take this shit seriously. With whoever has been stalking us for months, and these comments, I'm worried."

Courtney paced the room. Her show, her platform, was supposed to be her strength. But now, it felt like a vulnerability.

Like danger.

For some reason, Courtney glanced at Sakura, now somewhat recovered, watching her with wide, concerned eyes. She felt stupid for getting her involved. If someone was trying to harm her, at least she could do was get the girl to safety.

"Let's go. I'll take you home."

The city lights blurred past as Courtney navigated the Benz through the streets, the silence in the car filled only by the low hum of the engine and the occasional whoosh of passing cars. Sakura sat in the passenger seat, more alert now, her gaze fixed on the neon glow of the night.

"You didn't have to drive me all the way home," she said, breaking silence.

Courtney offered a half-smile, keeping her eyes on the road. "It's no problem. Just want to make sure you're safe."

Sakura nodded, then let out a sigh, her shoulders slumping as she let what was heavy off her chest. "I've got this nigga I'm fucking."

"I like you, but you don't have to talk just to be talking. I'm really good with silence."

"It's not like that. I mean, it's not about sex. Sometimes I wish it was because for real, he's all about the church so I don't know what the fuck he wants with me."

Courtney didn't know what to say.

"Anyway, he wants to put a ring on it, but..." Her voice trailed off, tangled in doubt.

"But what?" Courtney prompted, sensing there was more to the story.

"I'm a mess, Courtney. Pills, drink... It's like I'm in this hole and can't climb out. He doesn't really know. And I'm afraid if he finds out he'll leave me." Sakura confessed, her words spilling out with the weight of unshed tears.

Courtney's heart clenched. She'd seen this kind of pain, heard these confessions on air, but it was different up close, personal.

"There's something else you wanna tell me. So come clean."

"I'm still in love with my first love. Never got over him. He got with some girl and because he's not on the Internet, I don't even know where he is. If he thinks about me. You would think I would be able to move on since God gave me this dude, but he's...."

"Lavender?"

"Yes. Lavender." She took a deep breath. "But you, your show... it gives people like me hope. I wish I could've put him in his place. Told him how I really felt before he left. Maybe spit in his girlfriend's face.

Even though I only saw her from afar. But I was too afraid. The people on your show aren't."

Those words should've filled Courtney with pride, but instead, a tide of doubt washed over her.

They arrived at Sakura's place, a modest building with a flickering streetlight out front. She hesitated before getting out, turning to Courtney with earnest eyes. "I won't forget today. I'm not much, but if you need me, I'm here."

Courtney watched as she disappeared into the building.

As she drove back to her own home, the night seemed darker, the city more menacing. She needed to make a choice about what to do next. And whatever she chose, it had to be right.

The road ahead was uncertain, but one thing was clear, the next seven days would change everything.

CHAPTER TWO

Courtney stirred the pot on the stove, the aroma of seasoned chicken filling the kitchen. The window was open, and a cool breeze caressed her face as she thought about her day.

From her brother saying Tye Gates was getting out of prison, and the shit popping off at her studio, she was done.

The cutest thing she had going was the sound of laughter and the electronic beeps of a video game coming from the living room, where her son and her man, were locked in a virtual battle. She smiled at the normalcy of it, a contrast to the turmoil threatening to burn down her world.

Courtney wasn't a stranger to virtual beef. There were a lot of casters who wanted what she was building. If she continued to lock down the sponsors that she was getting she would be a millionaire before the end of the year. And not everybody wished for her greatness.

She was in her mind until Plazo's cell phone buzzed on the countertop. The man left his phone everywhere. It was clear he wasn't hiding anything. But since she was concerned about his recent mood shift, she instinctively picked it up. She hadn't been with Tye's ass in over fifteen years, but he still left a mark on her heart and caused her not to trust people.

Invading his privacy, her thumb swiped through messages before she could stop herself. She was deep in the act when Plazo walked in, catching her red-handed.

"Courtney, what you doing, bae?" He looked crushed.

She gazed up slowly, guilt washing over her. "I... I just—"

"What are you doing?" He stepped closer.

She placed the phone down. "I'm sorry, I-."

"But are you though?" Plazo cut in, disappointment etched on his face.

"Plazo—"

"I'm sick of this shit, Courtney. I'm sick of the distrust. I don't do shit except love on you. And because you want me to express what I'm not willing to say, you think I'm stepping out?"

She slumped into a chair; the phone forgotten. "If you would talk to me and tell me what's going on then I guess–"

"So you putting this ho shit on me?"

She was until he got mad. "No...it's just...with everything going on, the threats, and worrying about Lawson, I can't think straight."

She pulled the sympathy card. He knew what was up, but because he loved the woman it was approved.

Plazo leaned against the doorframe, his anger softening to concern. "Then maybe it's time to think of a Plan B."

"Not again."

He moved closer. "Ever since your brother showed up telling you about your son's father, shit been off. Maybe it's time for us to leave. Like we planned. I'm ready to–."

Their conversation was interrupted by a firm knock at the door.

Relieved someone was getting her out of a confrontation she started, she said, "I think that's my brother." She kissed him. "Let me check it out."

Before he allowed her to escape, he rested a hand on her lower back and said, "I'm here. Don't push me away by being insecure."

She nodded.

Rushing to the door, Posea, Courtney's brother, stepped in, his presence both comforting and a reminder of the world outside. The streets knew him as Run Mitchell. But she knew him as blood. His light skin was almost completely tatted up and despite his dark energy he was loyal as fuck to family.

"I checked on your ex." He hugged her and dapped Plazo. "He's still locked up, sis. No way he's behind the shit at your studio," Posea announced, trying to ease the tension.

A small wave of relief passed over Courtney, but it was fleeting.

"How you feel?"

"I guess I feel alright. But that doesn't take away what's been happening at the studio, does it?"

The smile washed off her brother and her man's faces.

"Hungry?" She asked.

"Me and my nigga beefin'. He ain't cook shit so you know I can eat."

"Well come in. It's almost ready."

They gathered at the dinner table, the food laid out, a picture of domesticity. But the air was heavy, each bite weighed down by unsaid fears. Dramas. Unseen enemies. If it wasn't Tye, who was behind the threats and shit?

The four of them ate mostly in silence, the usual banter replaced by worried glances and hushed tones.

Sensing that she was falling apart, Plazo reached for Courtney's hand, while Posea kept a protective eye on his nephew even as he sat at the table. The man's eyes literally roamed from window to window. Door to door. A quiet guardian in uncertain times.

There would be no resolutions tonight.

Wasn't shit resolved.

And Courtney doubted it ever would be.

Dear Diary,

Today was a bad day. I couldn't believe what was happening and I also couldn't believe that I almost lost my nigga doing too much by snooping through his phone. When I met him, and he told me I had blood on my clothes, I just knew he would never want to hear from me again.

After all it was gross.

Nasty.

But not only did he stay with me as if I was injured when he followed me back to my house, but he cooked for me later that night.

He was a woman's dream.

There were no baby mothers. No children unclaimed. He was a man building his insurance company and his construction company to stack up for the future.

And I lucked up.

And I fucked up too.

I fixed him good earlier tonight though. Stayed on my knees and sucked his dick until every creamy drop ran down my throat. Just like most men, he was weak when it came to the Head game.

Tye hurt me more than any man ever did, but he also taught me how to give head. That was the only useful thing he gave.

You didn't get up until he gave you the okay. Even if it meant choking to death.

When I was done, I laid in the bed next to him, wanting nothing but peace.

I got to find out what's going on. I need to know who's after me. For my son, my man and even my brother.

Posea had done so much for me even dropping bodies when I had my revenge plan against Tye, that I don't want him to have to give up more.

But murder may be my only direction if it's us versus them.

By T. STYLES

CHAPTER THREE

Courtney was driving down the street with Lawson in the passenger seat on the way to take him to his friend's house who played the quarterback position. And since Lawson was a wide receiver, they liked to throw the ball back-and-forth in the boy's backyard.

She carved out the time to be there with him because she never left him alone.

Luckily, he was preoccupied with his phone, and she knew she needed the moment to think. Earlier that day, Adrienne gave her all the reasons people may be after her and the podcast. But she cast a net so large that it was hard to pinpoint one person.

She decided to call her back. The moment Adrienne answered the phone, she said, "I think I'm gonna let it go."

"Let what go? You gonna let them take what you built?"

"It's not just about that. I'm thinking about Plazo and what we talked about. I have somebody who cares about me. Maybe I can start all over with him."

"But I don't have nobody to start over with. What about me?"

"Don't worry, whatever I do, there will be a place for you too."

Lawson looked over at her and she remembered she didn't want to say too much, especially if it meant them moving again.

Because despite Courtney's podcast being successful it wasn't the only location they lived in. They moved a lot. And every time she pulled her son out of school and away from his friends, for fear that Tye Gates was after them.

She considered it to be a necessary deed. But Lawson hated her for it.

"I don't think you should run. I think you should finally stand up, Courtney. You can do this shit."

"I just—"

Suddenly a car swiped the side of Courtney's Benz. Since she was less than a mile away from her destination, she was sort of relieved because she had gotten off the highway. If she was swiped on 95 it could've been more dangerous. She flung the phone down and quickly got over to the right of the road to park. The white pickup with dark tinted windows sped off. They didn't even stop to see if she was okay.

She knew then that it was done on purpose.

A few onlookers begin to approach the car. All of them asking if they were okay. She noted that she was fine and focused on Lawson.

"I'm so sorry, son. Are you good?"

"I'm fine, but are you?"

She placed her hand over her heart and tried to slow her breathing. "I'm good."

"Who was that?" He looked behind him and back at her.

"I don't know, son. But let me get you to D'Angelo's house. I'll call an Uber."

She grabbed her phone which was on the floor, and he touched her hand, "Ma, you can talk to me. I'm fifteen years old, I'm not a kid. I know something's up. I overheard you talking to Aunt Adrienne. I can handle—"

"I don't wanna hear that no more! About you being old. You're a kid! A fucking kid! Now start acting like it and stay in your fucking place!" He released her hand. "Let me get you to D'Angelo's house. Please!"

Courtney was smoking a cigarette.

She picked up the habit after she was released from prison when Tye took everything from her. But when he was incarcerated and she got her revenge, she let the habit go.

But now standing in D'Angelo's mother's front yard, she was on her second 'Jack' and losing her mind. She felt on edge. Weak and afraid. That was until she heard a speeding car down the block.

Without even seeing the vehicle, she knew it was Plazo. And sure enough as she continue to keep her eyes in the direction of the sound, she saw him. He whipped the Tesla to the side of the street and stormed out leaving the door open. Yanking the metal gate, he wrapped his arms around her and held her tightly.

"Are you good, babe?"

She nodded rapidly. "Yes, I'm fine! I just don't know what's going on!"

"What about Lawson? He good?"

"Yes. Everybody's okay."

"What is up with these niggas out here? How you going to hit a car and then roll out?! Make it make sense!" He was so angry he was shivering.

She was going to respond but heard another car and saw her brother pulling up. He didn't push in as quickly as Plazo, but she could tell he was trying to get at her just as fast. Once parked, he got out, closed Plazo's car door, pulled open the fence and walked into the yard.

He held his sister and released her. "Do you need anything, sis?"

"I think I'm good. I just want to find out what's going on. I don't know why this is happening. Especially if you tell me Tye is locked up."

"I promise to God he is."

Just then the front door opened, and Ms. Jackson exited. She approached with well-meaning intentions. But it was almost as if she walked into Courtney's living room because they all were pissed.

"Courtney, let me handle the kids. You need to sort this out, whatever it is."

Courtney shook her head, her voice steady, her resolve clear. "Appreciate you, but no. My place is here, with my son. This is non-negotiable. But, if you got a problem with us being here, I could always leave."

"Of course not. I just want to make things easy. Considering what just happened." She looked at the other two. "You all can come in if–."

"This is fine," Plazo said, shaking her hand. "We appreciate your hospitality though."

She nodded and walked away.

"We should leave." Plazo focused on his girl.

"She's going to be fine. She—"

"I'm talking about out of town. I played this game with you and I'm no longer willing to do it, bae. Don't put me in this position where I'm at work on them ladders having to wonder if my woman is fine."

Posea eyed her warily agreeing with Plazo. He was a real ass nigga, and he didn't want her to fuck it up. "Court, this isn't the time to be stubborn. The man is saying that it's not worth it and I agree. I pushed some things to the side so I can be with you at the studio, but even I can't watch you forever."

She looked at them both. Taking a deep breath, she gazed down and slowly rose her head. "Lawson thinks I'm weak. He thinks I'm not a fighter."

"I know you lying." Her brother said. "You are the strongest–."

"I'm not strong! I spent the last few years running!" She looked at Plazo. "And I would have left with you in a heartbeat if I didn't hear him say those words when I dropped him off at school. If I didn't see the fear in his eyes. I don't know what I'm going to do but for some reason I don't think the answer is running. Not this time."

The two men looked at one another.

Plazo took a very deep inhale. The kind that stopped the breath for a moment. After exhaling, he said, "Then what's the plan, bae? If you stay here what is the fucking plan?!"

"I don't know."

CHAPTER FOUR

The rain pounded on Courtney's studio as she sat in her car and looked at the door. She was driving a rental because the body shop had no time frame on when her insurance company would approve her claim. Also when it would be completed.

She didn't care what she was driving. It wouldn't help her out of her current predicament. She was looking for answers. Answers on where to start. And answers on where things may end.

When she was as calm as she was going to be, she pushed the door open and entered her studio. Adrienne and Keisha were waiting. Walking up to them, she said, "Okay let me see the emails."

Keisha and Adrienne looked at one another.

"Are you sure you want to do this?" Keisha asked.

"I'm with her. You told us not to let you—"

"I need to know who my enemies are. No I don't like to see negative comments, but if I'm going to run or stay I need to know what I'm dealing with first."

Adrienne and Keisha looked at one another and they all walked into Keisha's office. After logging onto the assistant's computer, she saw email after email from those who loved her podcast and many more from those who hated her. Hearing how some people despised her caused her stomach to churn and she was wondering if she had made a mistake by looking at such negativity.

But she stayed.

Focused.

And then something stood out.

There were many more hateful messages from her peers.

Two podcasters in particular who had done many things to try and get her banned from the best platforms due to not being able to compete. One of the podcasters didn't get a large sponsorship from a cell phone company. It was privately owned and they had a limited budget. After interviewing them both, they thought Courtney's podcast would help them reach their intended market better. It was the same story with the other podcast. For some reason many of the companies pit the three of their shows against one another.

And it worked.

At one time or another, they sent some of the most hateful messages Courtney had ever received from a human being. Especially since she had only been in their company twice at a podcast networking event.

With Adrienne by her side, they collected so many contacts that ended in advertising and sponsorship, that Courtney was able to buy a new house and that Benz. Even Adrienne was able to get a new Tesla.

The two podcasters were livid.

From that point on weird things would happen. She would order food, and when the company would drop it off seals would be broken. One time she ordered a sandwich and it looked like spit was on the burger. She couldn't put it directly onto them, but she had no problems prior to meeting them at those events.

"Are you seeing what I'm seeing?" Courtney questioned.

Keisha and Adrienne looked at one another.

"I do." Adrienne smiled. "I think you got your answer."

"I think I know our next move too," Courtney said.

When Courtney walked into her son's room she saw all of his suitcases leaned against the wall.

Frowning for a moment she walked over to the closet and saw all but three outfits on hangers. Not only was this unusual but Lawson never cleaned his room.

"This is different." Walking over to him she leaned against the wall. "We're doing this now?"

"I mean we're leaving right?" He grabbed the controller on his game and began to play. "That's what we always do."

"You think you know everything. But, I'm not going anywhere this time."

He placed the controller down and looked over at her. "What you mean? What changed?"

She nodded and took a deep breath. "That's a good question, and I want to be honest with you. If we stay–"

"You mean if we fight."

"If we fight, Lawson, I don't know what that means for our peace. I don't even know who's after me or who is trying to ruin my life."

"You think it's my dad?"

"Like I said I don't know. And because I don't know I may bring things into our lives that don't need to be here. And I want you to really understand this, Lawson. As much as you can as a child."

He turned his body to face her. "Six years ago..."

She frowned.

"Six years ago was the last time I was at peace. We had the apartment, and it was just the two of us. We didn't have a yard or anything like that, but I was grateful."

"Grateful, huh?"

"Yes. Because I knew you were somewhat happy. In my mind we haven't had peace since then, mom. So I'm not concerned or scared. If you want to leave I'm with you. I just want us to at least try. I even gave this girl name Lola my number. And I think she's going to call me. But it won't be worth it if we aren't here."

Courtney smiled knowing what that meant.

"Let's at least try to be normal."

"Again, I want to make sure you understand. It means if we stay, we fight, Lawson. What that looks like on my end is that I may not always be happy. I may not always know what to say. And I don't know what will come our way."

"Do you need me to put on gloves?"

She walked over to him and he stood up and hugged her tightly. "No, but I do need you to unpack because we aren't going anywhere."

CHAPTER FIVE

I t was Plazo's time to host the meeting in his crib. In attendance was his girl, Posea, and Adrienne. He set the table at his place, a spread of soul food that filled the room with the comforting aromas of home-cooked collard greens, fried catfish, dirty rice, and sweet cornbread.

A playlist of smooth R&B classics hummed in the background, setting a relaxed mood despite the tension in the air. They all sat with drinks in hand. Plazo with his bourbon neat, Courtney sipping on a gin and juice, while Posea nursed a cold beer and Adrienne sipped on a glass of red wine.

As they dug into the meal, the conversation turned to the task at hand. Courtney, her voice steady despite the gravity of their discussion, laid out her suspicions.

"My plan is simple. Just like they're trying to ruin my business, scare me so I can run and they can have a leg up, I'm going to dismantle everything they love!"

Adrienne smiled but Courtney's brother and man weren't too keen. They had never heard her speak like she did in that moment. Sure she gave others advice about their lives on her podcast, but she never reacted this way when it came to her own life.

"I need you to be clear." Plazo said.

"I thought about this for a long time. Over the past few days actually. And I narrowed things down to the following groups of people who may be fucking with me. Leaving shit on my doorstep, scratching my car. All the shit I let slide. Now I don't know if they're responsible but—"

"Hold up...if they not the ones then why move on them?" Her brother asked.

"Because they have already done plenty of shit to me online too. You should read the messages I got from them. I never said anything."

Her brother nodded his head. "Then let's hear it. Who are they? Because a foul against you is a foul against me."

"And you already know I'm with whatever," Adrienne added.

They all looked at Plazo. "I'm here for you. But I'm going to always tell you the truth. I'm not feeling this one bit. I want to take my lady away from all this. Move down south like we talked about."

"And y'all can still do all that," Adrienne responded. "Just not right now."

"I know you want what we discussed. I'm just asking you to ride with me in the moment."

"What you're saying doesn't make sense. You want to go at two groups of people because they may have done something."

"Do you ever wonder why I get up extra early? I know you always thought it was to write in my diary if I forgot. But it's because I have to go outside every morning to make sure something weird is not on my front step. Or if the car is scratched I have Lawson get in on the other side, even if it's awkward, just so he won't see it. I'm tired of being afraid. If this won't work, you'll get what you want, Plazo. What we want. Just let me stand up for myself finally." She took a deep breath and looked at the others.

"I just don't see how podcasters can be this toxic."

"Oh, they not no ordinary casters." Adrienne said. "These are hood niggas masquerading behind a microphone. And, like I told Courtney, once they find out we gonna do what we do, they may send everybody!"

"Well you know that's where I come in at," Posea said. "If it's going to be that, let it be that."

Courtney took a deep breath. "So this is what we have right now. First up, we've got the *'Mommy Moves'* podcast. They claim they are about the single baby mama hustle. Giving out tips on how to not pay for shit especially childcare, but I heard they may be scammers. As a matter of fact, I got some leads out there that can vouch for it."

Adrienne took a deep sip. "But what about '*The Glam Girls*'?"

"What the fuck is that?" Posea asked.

"I know it sounds stupid. They on they pretty bitches rule shit. Claiming they don't have to reach in their purses to pay for nothing. Not the clothes on their backs. The houses they live in. The cars they drive. But I know something else is up. And I got a few ideas on how to find out. The streets talk. I just need to lock them in."

Posea leaned back, taking a big bite of his catfish. "You forgetting one group."

"Who?"

"The niggas that's rolling with Tye remember?"

"But you said Ty was still locked up."

Plazo shook his head, his face filled with concern. "If that dude still in jail, and they fucking with you for no reason, that's some next-level bitch shit."

Courtney's mind was a whirlwind of names and potential motives. "I won't take them off the table. But I'll start with the two I know hate me. And have fired shots at me. And that I constantly let slide."

As they continued to strategize, it was clear that they would need each other. And Courtney, with the support of her closest allies felt things shaping up. Maybe she wasn't weak after all.

CHAPTER SIX

Dear Diary,
　　I can't tell you how good it feels when he's inside me. It's not just about how he makes me feel.

Or about busting a nut.

Or cumming.

Or any of the terms used to express the explosion that seems to take over my body when we fuck. It's more about how he looks at me. And how he manages to make me feel strong and sexy, even when I don't feel it myself.

We just finished making love and it's still on my mind. The scent of him. The feel of him. Before doing anything he turned the light on by the side of the bed. Something he did 80 percent of the time to see me. To see how I looked at him.

Then he massaged my toes. I mean each one. As if he needed to touch every inch of my body to survive.

My ankles, my calves, my legs, my thighs. About that time I wanted the dick so badly, I would do almost anything for it. But he made me wait. And went up to my belly with soft, gentle touches.

By T. STYLES

It always feels unnatural when he goes there though.

Like, he's touching my heart physically with his hands and squeezing it between his fingers. While he looks at it as an extension of myself, my belly always feels too round.

But to him, it's my body and he wants all of it.

Next, he goes up my breasts, but this time he doesn't use his fingertips. He uses his lips. He kisses around them at first before gently sucking the nipples. By this time, I was so wet I could feel my juices dripping onto the bed beneath me.

Dampening the yellow sheets.

When he does this, it takes everything in me not to reach an orgasm because he's so romantic.

Soft kisses on my neck.

My lips.

I always get excited around this point because I know that soon, he'll be inside me.

Tunneling.

Easing.

And just as I thought, he pushed into me. Shoveling behind my lower back, so that he can get a good grip to push in and out. Over and over. Wetter and wetter.

Harder.

I don't want this to ever end.

This felt too good.

And yet tonight wasn't about sex. At least not to me.

He had a reason.

Something is up, Diary. As I'm writing these pages when I feel his warm breath behind me, instead of him facing outward, like he normally did when it was time to rest, I knew he wanted to talk.

Let me get it over with.

She closed her diary.

She rolled over and faced him.

And in the stillness of the night, with the soft hum of the city's heartbeat whispering through the open window, Courtney and Plazo found themselves staring at one another. He was more intense than she was.

The quietness of her bedroom, a contrast to the chaos that had become their lives. The faint glow of streetlights casted shadows across the room, painting a picture of an urban night.

Plazo's voice was a soft rumble in the darkness, "You felt good."

She smiled.

What did he really want to say?

"Bae, let's make that move to Texas. Build that house we always talked about? Start clean."

"Repetition won't change my mind." Courtney's silhouette was outlined by the city lights as she propped herself up on one elbow.

"A few days ago you wanted to talk. So let's do it. Let me tell you what's been on my mind."

"Listening."

"You've been different ever since your brother told you Tye maybe getting out of prison. And I feel like the end of what we're trying to build together is about to happen. Before we even start, baby."

"I don't understand."

"Let me be clear. You're still in love with him."

"No, I'm not! Why would I love somebody who caused me so much drama and—."

"You do love him. And I'm not insecure. But the stories you told me about him leaves me to believe that he still has control of your mind. So let's build a future and leave all this other shit behind!" Plazo's unease was real and she felt it on every inch of her soul. "We got enough stacked to live good for a while without looking over our shoulders. Don't need to be chained to this city...to the drama."

"No." It was the only thing she could muster.

"Your nigga just said he trying to build with you and you tell him no?"

"Would you prefer I lie?" She whispered, a tear rolling down her face.

Silence.

"Turn around..." He told her.

She did.

His warm body pressed against her back as they settled into an embrace, the kind that spoke volumes without a word being uttered.

"I thought we were talking."

"You have your mind made up, Courtney. So I just want to remember the moment when I warned you."

CHAPTER SEVEN

Courtney sipped coffee in the breakroom of her office, the smell of fresh brew mingling with the scent of printer ink. Her brother, Posea, leaned against the counter, his expression serious.

"I know you don't know her, but she's ready."

"Are you sure?" Courtney raised an eyebrow, her mind flashing to images of her cousin on her father's side.

"You gotta trust me sometimes."

Yo-Yo, a striking figure in the streets, was as confident as they came, her light skin marred by acne scars but her presence was undiminished by it. She was the type who owned every room she walked into, and her street smarts were as renowned as her boldness and real niggas fucked with her for it.

"Because she real deep out here in these streets, Posea. And this may be too boring for–"

"It's what you need. *She's* what you need. Especially if you still unwilling to show your face."

"I wouldn't be able to show my face here no way. They know me."

"Even more reason why we need, Yo-Yo. Plus she's got ears everywhere, and she's smart, Court. More than people give her credit for. And whether you refused to fuck with everybody else on your father's side or not, she's still family. One of my favorite people. So I'm vouching for her."

"You're right. Set it up."

Posea's grin was priceless. He wanted her to meet more members of her family. Since all she had ever known was him.

"Yo-Yo's gonna be a game changer, Court. You'll see." He hugged her and walked away.

Courtney's sleek Benz stood out against the gritty backdrop of the DC projects as she drove by. She navigated through the crowded streets, the car's purr drowned out by the laughter and shouts on almost every block. Go-Go music boomed from parked cars, pulsing through the air, interrupted by the occasional honking horn.

When she made it to the address, she pulled up in front of a an apartment building, its exterior worn but standing proud in the midst of chaos. Before she could even honk, the front door of the building swung open, and Yo-Yo emerged, a vision straight out a music video.

Three men followed just as fine as they wanted to be in different shades of brown and what each of them had in common were the beards that covered their faces.

Yo-Yo was draped in jewelry—Cuban links, nameplates, and diamonds that caught the sunlight and sent it scattering in all directions. She moved with a confidence that commanded attention, her entourage keeping close behind.

As Yo-Yo slid into the passenger seat of the Benz, her bodyguards took up positions nearby, their eyes scanning the area with practiced vigilance.

Courtney locked the door and got straight to the point.

"Hey, cuzo!" Yo-Yo said. The moment she got into her car she seemed to be chiming from all angles. Who kept their cell on ring anyway?

"How many of them do you have?"

"Sorry, let me cut it off."

Courtney was done already and the woman had yet to say anything. "Can you handle this, Yo-Yo? It's not small stakes."

"Of course, cuz," Yo-Yo replied, her voice smooth and assured. "You know I got you. You should have come to me from the rip. I would have put all them fake bitches in they place."

"It's not like that!"

"That's not what your brother told me. He made it like you had beef and so you needed my help."

"Yes, but not really."

"Now you confusing me."

"I have beef but not like how you have in the streets. Like no guns are involved. Nobody's trying to kill me."

"Then you ain't got beef."

"What are you talking about?"

Yo-Yo positioned her body to look into her eyes. "If you answer yes to all or two of these questions you need me."

"Go 'head."

"Are you afraid? Are you able to sleep at night? Are you worried about your son? Is this fucking with your bag?"

Courtney sat back and nodded her head yes to everything.

"Just like I thought, you got beef."

"But, I don't think it's going to take long when they get a taste of their own medicine."

"On the phone you said you wrote down what you need?"

She raised her hand and a sheet of paper was folded in her palm. "It's all here. Just tear it up when you're done."

She looked at the paper then tucked it into her bra.

The conversation shifted, Yo-Yo suggesting, "You know...you should let my lil cuzo come hang with us sometime. Get to know his grandfather's side and his cousins. My sons. It's not just about Posea."

Courtney stiffened at the suggestion, her protective instincts flaring up. She glanced around the block and felt like everybody she could see had ill will in their hearts. There was no fucking way she was letting her son stay there. "I appreciate it, but no. He's better off where he is."

"You afraid of who you are. And that's a shame."

"I don't need to be judged."

"No judgment. Just observation." Yo-Yo's disappointment was palpable, but she let it slide with a shrug, an unspoken understanding between them.

Despite their differences, Courtney found herself drawn to something in Yo-Yo, a raw authenticity that was both intimidating and intriguing. Handing over a wad of cash for the task ahead, Courtney watched, frozen, as Yo-Yo rolled down the window and passed it to one of her men without a second thought.

"What is you doing?"

"Giving one of my Baby fathers the money to put up. Why?"

"Are you tripping?"

"Nah," Yo-Yo said, seeing the look on Courtney's face. "I trust my baby fathers. Got three, and they ain't going nowhere. Me either."

Courtney marveled silently at her cousin's confidence, her ease with trust, a major difference from her own guarded nature. "I don't trust anyone," Courtney admitted, the words heavy with the weight of her reality.

"But your brother said you gotta man."

"I do. But I'm always feeling like at some point he will leave. Despite what he says."

Yo-Yo nodded, understanding. "Must be scary, living in a world where you can't trust nobody. But you can trust me, cuz."

Silence.

Their meeting ended with Yo-Yo pulling Courtney into an unexpected hug, her embrace firm and warm.

Courtney wanted to fight at first but she changed her mind and went with it. Besides, it felt real.

As she exited the car, she yelled back, "I'll hit up the girl Sakura like you said. But I may not need her for this part of the plan. Besides, I'm better alone."

"Your call."

"Don't worry. You with family now. I got you!"

Courtney watched her cousin blend back into the vibrant tapestry of the projects. In Yo-Yo's world, trust was a currency as valuable as any diamond she wore. And as Courtney drove away, she couldn't help but wonder what it would be like to live with such unshakeable confidence.

Because she knew if Lawson didn't call her on her weakness, she would've never stood up.

When Courtney pulled up in front of her house she walked inside and tossed all of her clothing by the front door. Something she often did when she wanted to get the weight of the world off. Something she also did when her son wasn't around. But when she strolled in this time, she saw her brother sitting on the sofa, staring outward.

"What the—." She covered her breasts.

"Sorry, sis, I let myself in. Something I do from time to time to make sure everything good in the house."

Courtney was surprised to see him and she could tell by the look in his eyes that there was something bothering him. Lowering her body, she quickly got dressed.

"I heard the meeting went good with Yo-Yo." He looked at her.

She nodded. "What's going on? With you?"

As they sat in her living room Posea's tough facade crumbled. "My boyfriend's gone, Court," he said, his voice strained. "He says it's too much for him."

"What's too much for him?" She sat next to him on the sofa. "We haven't even started anything yet."

"It's not just this moment. It's all the moments."

Courtney reached across and touched his hand. "I'm sorry, P. You okay? Can I do anything?"

He shrugged, and a deep sigh escaped him. "It's not just about that. It's about you."

"Me?"

"I saw Plazo's face. He's almost done. And this path you're on its a dark road that leads to loneliness."

Courtney laughed, but there was no humor in it. "Coming from you, that's rich. What, you a saint now?"

Posea shook his head, and his expression turned serious. "I'm telling you this because I know how bad it can get. And I did some background on both of those podcasters. *The Glam Girls*, they out here. I'm out here." He leaned in. "But you ain't got to be."

The room fell silent. Courtney looked at her brother, seeing the genuine worry etched on his face. She wrapped her arms around him tightly.

"Listen, I'm grown. And I know you love me, but it's important you know that." She whispered, but her voice wavered slightly. "And I'm tired of the men in my life trying to make me feel differently. If you don't want no problem between us, leave it alone."

Posea hugged her back, his embrace protective. "Understood."

He got up and walked out the door.

CHAPTER EIGHT

Courtney orchestrated a plan to expose *The Glam Girls*, and the key to its success was her cousin Yo-Yo. Under the guise of a glamorous guest, Yo-Yo walked into the party like she owned the bitch and it didn't take her long to spot the hostesses of the hour.

First there was Brianna, known as Bree in her circle. She grew up facing the harshest realities of Baltimore's inner-city life but was determined to rise above her situation. Her motto was where there's a Pussy, there's a way. Medium height with a commanding presence, she carried herself with authority. Her hair was usually styled with flowing waves and her accessories were statements...large hoop earrings, layered necklaces, and an array of rings on her fingers.

Her business partner, Jasmine, who was affectionately called Jazz, faced a turbulent upbringing herself in one of Baltimore's most notorious neighborhoods. Raised by a single mother who worked multiple jobs, she found herself alone and vulnerable to the influences of street life. Luckily her friend Bree had a plan and a hustle, and so she joined her podcast.

The rest was money.

Slightly shorter than Bree, her fashion sense was more toned down. Her hair was in a bob and her makeup accentuated her naturally beautiful features.

As the girls, popped bottles and popped shit, they had no idea that there was an enemy amongst them.

And that person, in Courtney's honor, mingled through the crowd, snapping pictures on the side, she saw things that fucked her up but nothing that nobody really gave a fuck about.

So she did a little more snooping. Toward the back of the club were mostly shadows, like a vignette blackening things out. On the surface, everything looked normal, but Yo-Yo was deep in the streets and knew something else was going on. She just needed to see better.

And so while everyone drank from bottles with brown or white liquor inside, she moved toward the edges to get a closer look.

On face value it looked like men and women were enjoying themselves. But when she started paying closer attention, she noticed every other dude had a female on his lap. The female would be bouncing as if she's dancing but when she squinted, she saw what was really going on.

They were fucking straight out in the open.

For all to see.

Was this what *The Glam Girls* called using their pretty privilege? When they were actually using their pussies instead.

Curious as fuck, she snapped all kinds of pictures. Some blurry. Some grainy. And some as clear as if she'd been next to them herself. But who cared about a whore and the nigga who paid them?

She wanted more.

Something that held weight.

Because at the end of the day, her eyes were sharp, and her mind was focused. She was there to gather proof that *The Glam Girls'* lifestyle of getting things for free based on their looks was a sham.

So, she didn't stop there. She discreetly recorded conversations, looking for any slip-up or confession that would reveal the truth. Her phone, hidden in her elegant clutch, was her tool in this game of deception.

Before long, she found herself sitting across from Jasmine's cousin, a young girl who was a bit too loose-lipped, especially after Yo-Yo bought her a couple of rounds. The girl was clearly feeling Yo-Yo's swagger and street charm, hanging onto her every word.

By T. STYLES

After about 10 minutes talking about the audience she said, "You're Jasmine's cousin, right?"

The mood seemed ruined for the girl. "So, you want to talk about them like everybody else?"

"I wanna talk to you." Sensing the girl needed attention she came up with a plan. "I'm not into everything they're about anyway."

The girl smiled. "Really?"

"Nah. I don't buy it. They phony. They really want people to believe that they don't spend money on anything? Everything is paid for by dudes?"

The girl looked around and leaned closer. "You're right, it's all a lie. They got some niggas backing them." The cousin, tipsy and talkative, didn't hold back. "Jazz and Bree both fuck with some dealers from DC who need their money clean. Nair one of them niggas faithful and they can't stand either one of them hoes. The moment they don't need them no more, they gonna get rid of them. Murder or Muting them out...it's the same."

"You sound like you scared."

"Of Roberto and Victor? Fuck yea."

Yo-Yo was recording everything she said.

"I knew I fucked with you." She leaned in closer. "Now tell me more."

As the night wore on, Yo-Yo played it cool, letting the cousin spill everything. She almost felt bad for her. By the time they called it a night, Yo-Yo had both them niggas names and digits. The cousin was all too eager to give them up, thinking she was impressing Yo-Yo in the process.

"Well, don't forget to call me," Yo-Yo said referring to her fake number. "I gotta get out of here, but we gonna get some drinks later."

"I'll call you tomorrow."

"Bet." Eager to get at her cousin, Yo-Yo strutted out the club, confidence riding high.

But the night had other plans.

Just as she reached the faintly lit lot where her vehicle was parked, a sleek navy-blue car pulled up. Out stepped *The Glam Girls*, Jazz and Bree, their faces twisted in anger.

"Yo, who the fuck are you? And why you spending so much time rapping to my cousin?" Jasmine asked.

"Bitch, you talking too much!" Bree said.

Before Yo-Yo could react, Bree lunged forward, her hands clawing for Yo-Yo's phone. The air was charged with tension, a scuffle erupting in the shadows of the streetlights. Yo-Yo fought hard, but it was two against one. They were getting the best of her no doubt, and at least two times in a 5-minute fight she lost consciousness.

Yo-Yo was doing her best to get her equilibrium straight. If it was a one on one, she would've whooped that bitch's ass. But both took turns, scratching her and hitting her in the face and head. She was outmatched.

Now she was lying flat on the concrete face up.

Breathing heavily, Jasmine said, "I don't know who you are, but I bet not see your fucking face again!"

When it was all said and done they had taken her phone and dipped right back into the car they exited.

Bruised Yo-Yo walked up to a dude who was shocked when he saw the condition of her yellow face. "You got a car?" She touched her bloody lip.

"Yeah, cutie. But what happened to you?"

"Take me where I'm going and I'll pay you when I get there."

"You ain't got to do all that." He picked her up.

Back at Courtney's studio, the planned meeting place, she was shocked to see her cousin fucked up on the other side of the glass door.

"Yo-Yo, what the fuck happened?" Courtney's voice was laced with concern as she hurried over. "Did you do this?" She asked the man.

"What I look like?" He raised his hands in the air.

"It wasn't him!" Yo-Yo interrupted. "He helped me out."

He looked at both of the ladies suspiciously, and said, "I gotta hit it back to Baltimore. But I got your number now. I'ma call you and check up with you later." He quickly exited the building before the police came, and they tried to pin some shit on him.

Courtney sat next to her. "Cuz, what happened?!"

Yo-Yo recounted the ambush, her words punctuated with anger. "They fucking jumped me. Took my damn phone too."

Courtney's eyes hardened. Using tissue from the dispenser, she gently tended to her wounds.

"But they don't know Yo-Yo like they think they know." She had a sinister smile on her face.

"What you mean?"

"I always have two phones on me at all times. Sometimes three."

Courtney grinned remembering all of the ringing when she first met her. "So you saying you got something for me?"

"I sure do. I told you, you should've been fucking with me from the gate. Now you know." She took a deep breath. "It's going to be too easy to take them down. To make them look like phonies because that's what they are. But if we're going to do this, you going to have to leave the studio. I got a feeling that them niggas is gonna be a handful. This girl I was talking to said they use Jasmine and Bree for washing their money. She also said they were killers."

"That's probably cap. At the same time, Posea told me about them."

"I don't want nothing to happen to you. I'm not saying you have to give the spot away. But I wouldn't host no podcast here for the next couple of weeks. Maybe months."

"I got a new place. It's a smaller office. Two rooms. But it'll do. It may not seem like it, but I have a plan. Now let's get these bruises cleaned up for real."

CHAPTER NINE

The night was enveloped in a relentless downpour. The streets, usually busy and loud, now quiet, and serene with the exception of raindrops. Only the occasional flash of headlights disturbed the tranquility.

Inside her apartment, Jasmine rose from her knees after wiping the corners of her mouth after sucking her boyfriend's dick. She did it so much that he could never last longer than 60 seconds, but she was just happy mostly that it was over.

With him knocked out, she decided to freshen up. She was only in there about 15 minutes. So she was surprised he was sitting on the edge of the bed staring at her. The lamp was on and highlighted his light brown skin. His hair tamed in a field of cornrows to the back.

"What's wrong with you?" She released the towel and proceeded to lotion her body.

She was doing her thighs when he said, "Let me ask you something...you've been telling people my business?"

She moved to the other side. "What?" She giggled. "You sound crazy."

"I'm asking you a serious question."

"Roberto, why would I tell anybody your business? Make it make sense before you accuse me." She did her elbows next.

"Why am I hearing that you letting people know what we do in the street?"

"Now I know you lying. You have known me forever. Since when have you known me to do something like that?" She grabbed a red nightgown from her top drawer and slipped it over her naked body.

"So, my brother lying too? Telling me that you and Bree running around saying that y'all washing our money with the podcast?"

Jazz backed up slowly into the wall.

She felt sick.

"All this questioning me like you crazy is making me—"

"Bitch, don't play with me!"

She jumped when she heard the thunder in his voice. "You scaring me right now."

He rose and walked over to her. "I got three different people I trust coming up to me. Each one of them saying that your cousin was recorded saying our business is being cleaned by that podcast."

"I don't know about all of that because—."

"If you tell me, it's not your fault again, I'ma drop you. That girl is your family. Your people. Just because she blood don't mean she should be knowing about my money."

She took a deep breath.

"When you first said you wanted my help to launch that podcast I was all in. Even put you up in this apartment. Bought that car. Like for real taking care of you. And all I ask is that you keep your mouth closed and don't let this shit come back on me. And what you do? Go against everything we talked about. And now it ain't working for me no more."

"What you trying to say?"

"This shit over!" He slapped his hands together causing a sound to rip through the night. "The podcast is done! If you do shit right maybe you can start fresh. Either way, I don't give a fuck."

Her eyes widened. "Roberto, I can't do that."

"Hold up, didn't you just hear what I said?"

"I did, but I can't do that. You're asking me to stop my bread and butter."

"Oh, so you can stop mine? I already gotta deal with my friends thinking that the lifestyle you got is from you letting other niggas smash. All that pretty privileged shit you be pumping. Half of the time you don't wash your ass right, which is why I get you to suck my dick instead. Putting all that lotion on, but not using soap."

"I know you lying!"

"I ain't going to jail fucking with you! I'll see all y'all buried first! You, your cousin, Bree, and anybody else involved."

She felt sick. At the same time she was tired of letting him push her over. "I'm sorry, but no."

"No?" His head tilted to the right like a Pitbull, trying to understand.

"I won't do it. All that's gonna happen if you decide you don't want me no more is you gonna kick me out. Like you've done before. And I'm not gonna have any money to take care of myself."

He laughed. "You know what, that may be true. But that's also the price you have to pay for fucking with the nigga like me. But let me be clear. You're done with that little podcast."

She was trembling. "Let me hear it. If you say this thing happened, let me hear it."

"So my word not good, no more?"

"You just let me suck your dick. Came in my mouth. And then told me to give up my dreams. So yes, I need to hear it. And I know you may beat my ass and all that other shit but I still don't care."

He shook his head and dragged his hand down his face. The fact that she was pressing him so hard annoyed him greatly. He felt she was buying into that privileged shit. Feeling all confident about herself and what not. At the same time, he would give her what she wanted for the moment, besides it wouldn't matter anyway, because he always, always got his way.

Grabbing his cell phone from the side table, he played the message that was sent to him from his brother from an unknown caller.

She heard her cousin speaking in great detail about her business. About washing money. The longer she listened the angrier she got. She knew her cousin had a big mouth, but this took the cake.

Still, now Jazz was hip on why he was mad. And she had a feeling she knew exactly where he got the information. The girl they beat up outside the club. The thing was she knew she took her phone. So how was she able to still give this information?

When the message was over, he placed the phone back on the table. Then he walked closer and massaged her shoulders roughly. Something he always did when he wanted to show who was more powerful.

"The podcast is over."

"Please, baby don't do this."

"Over. Do you understand me?" His voice deeper.

She nodded.

He walked towards the door. "Good, now. put some clothes on and make me something to eat. Your head wasn't as official. So now I gotta go beat my dick."

Bree was sitting in her living room drinking Hennessy from the bottle when Jazz came over.

"The door was unlocked so I let myself in."

Slowly, she rose. And they both stared at one another before saying a word. The podcast had become their identity. Nobody in either of their families thought they would make the money that they were making.

Sure, there boyfriends provided most of the access they claimed they got based on their looks. At the same time, the sponsorships and everything else came from their hustle, their grind.

"I've been writing down every number that called that phone." Bree said, "I've been making sure that every single one gets written down."

Jasmine nodded. "As well you should. But what we gonna do after that shit though? Because somebody has to pay if we don't have our podcast." She paused. "Like who was the girl? What she want with us?"

"Let me ask you something, Jazz, you still fucking with your ex? Because that bitch is crazy. She told you that."

She stepped closer. Her warm breath on Bree's face. "Is Victor here?"

"Would not have asked you if he was. Now answer the question."

"Are you tripping? Roberto would destroy me!"

"Then who is she? Who goes all out their way to record conversations? We not no politicians."

"How do I know it's not because of you?" Jazz said.

The room was intense. Not knowing who was after them was causing them to not trust one another. And they had been ride or die even before the podcast.

Silence.

By T. STYLES

For a moment, they were making a decision without words. Were they really going to fight each other?

"I think we should calm down before we do something we can't take back," Bree said.

"Me too. Until we find out something else, let's just record the numbers. When we're done, we'll go from there."

"Nah, I know what we can do right now. Let's get your cousin over here! Now!" Bree lowered her gaze.

When Jasmine's cousin walked through the door, she was shocked by the mood. Normally when she would come over they would drink and talk about the latest fashion, gossip, and anything else under the sun. But now they were looking at her as if they wanted to jump her.

"What's wrong with y'all?"

"Why would you talk about my business?" Jasmine asked.

"I didn't talk about your business!"

"You have been talking about our business!" Bree said. "I know because we heard your voice."

"Are you crazy?"

Jasmine shoved her clear across the room. And when she got up, she shoved her again. When she got up another time, she shoved her so hard, the back of her head indented Bree's wall.

"Hold up," Bree yelled. "Don't mess up my fucking house."

Jasmine waved her hand and rolled her eyes. Focusing back on her cousin, she said, "You have a problem running your mouth. And I'm sick of it."

"She's right." Bree said. "You've done this before."

"Now, since you were running your mouth, you gotta make shit right. The person you was with at the club. Who was getting you those drinks. Who is she? Light skin girl with acne on her face."

Her eyes widened and she backed up against the wall while still remaining seated. "Hold up, she recorded me?"

"Yes."

"I'm sorry. I was drinking too much and—"

"I don't care about all that shit. What I care about is who you were talking to."

"Her name is Yo-Yo."

"Yo-Yo?" Jasmine said.

"Yes. She's in the streets." It was clear she was on her stan shit because she was smiling so hard. "Got these baby daddies that would do anything for her. Like I think she still in a relationship with each of them. I mean they don't fuck each other, but they act like brothers. Y'all never heard of Yo-Yo?"

Bree looked at Jasmine who walked over to them. "No."

"How y'all claim y'all connected and don't know—
."

"Don't get smart," Jasmine yelled.

Bree lowered her height, "I want you to tell me everything you know. Don't hold back shit."

CHAPTER TEN

The sun blazed down mercilessly on the bustling streets, turning the asphalt into a shimmering mirage. Heatwaves radiated from the pavement and the air was thick and heavy, carrying the scent of street food and the distant sound of laughter.

Inside Courtney's house where the air was blasting, she sat with Sakura, and Yo-Yo going over details. Sakura was listening to Courtney although Yo-Yo had her full attention.

"I'm sorry, but I can't be rude. At the same time it's killing me. I have to know what happened to your face."

She shook her head. "It's the same thing that's gonna happen to yours if you don't listen to my cousin."

Sakura shrugged. "To be honest, I don't even care. I need some excitement right now." She twisted the cap on a bottle of vodka Courtney had on the table.

Courtney frowned. "What's wrong with you? You broke up with your boyfriend?"

"No, he still wants to be with me." She poured a hefty cup.

"So if you didn't break up with your nigga, what's the problem?" Yo-Yo persisted.

"My life going too well. I'm having my way. And I realized my way is not interesting enough."

Yo-Yo shook her head, but for some reason she understood exactly where the young girl was coming from.

Courtney stepped closer. "Are you sure your people are going to go along with part two of the plan, Sakura? Because I need them for this shit."

"Yeah, they're excited about it. They finally happy they're going to get money for stuff they be doing for free all day long. So why we wasting time, let's go." She drank everything in the cup.

It was in the late afternoon as Jasmine and Bree took off down the street. They couldn't wait to make it to the address that was given to them by a strange caller. Telling the girls to come right away, or else they would release the audio online. Possibly getting their boyfriends hemmed up with the fucking law. Whoever made the call didn't know it but Roberto and Victor were trailing behind the girls in another car, ready for war.

Although the strange caller said that the plan was to give them some information on Yo-Yo, their boyfriends wanted blood. And the girls wanted them to have it too.

"I think this the address right here," Bree who was driving said.

When they got to the apartment building, they pulled over, hopped out and looked around. Stepping in front of the building, and not knowing where to go Jasmine yelled upward, "We here! Where is that bitch Yo-Yo! And what does she want from us?"

People passed them by on the sidewalk as they continued to yell the same thing over and over to the top of their lungs.

Finally, after what seemed like forever, someone dropped a soda in front of them from the top floor. The metal crashed against the concrete and sizzled right in front of them. If they moved 1 inch, it would have hit one of them on the head. Looking up again, they saw somebody hanging out of the window.

It was Sakura.

As they continued to find out who she was, the sun blinded them momentarily. But eventually they saw the cute but strange girl's face.

"Who are you?" Jasmine said. "And where's Yo-Yo?"

"Don't worry about all that."

"Don't worry about that? You the one who invited us here, Jasmine continued. "If you not gonna hand over the girl, at least tell us what this is all about."

"How about I start asking some questions?"

"What you want to know, bitch?" Bree asked.

"Why you been fucking with my friend?"

Jasmine frowned. She was irritated already. "Again...who the fuck are you talking about? And why don't you come down here so we can hear each other better?"

Sakura giggled. "Nah, I'm good up here. Plus I see your little boyfriends in the car back there. Got them on camera with guns and everything."

They were caught.

The girls felt sick.

"Y'all gotta understand, I know somebody in every one of these apartment buildings on this block. So if you wanted to be slick, you shouldn't have even come. And just like they got guns aimed at me, there are about three windows with guns aimed at you. Nobody safe."

Jasmine and Bree didn't feel so confident anymore.

"Now, like I was saying, why are you fucking with my friend?"

"How about you tell me who your friend is, bitch?" Bree said. "We've been saying the same thing since we got here."

"Courtney. From *'An Ugly Girls Diary'* podcast."

Both of their jaws dropped. She was too square to do anything like this, so they almost didn't believe her.

"You telling me Courtney was behind all this? Brought pox mark face to my party?" Jasmine continued. "She ruined everything for this?"

"I'm waiting for an answer."

"Outside of spitting in her food that one time and fucking with that dude she liked, I didn't do nothing to that girl," Jasmine said.

"Me either. I didn't..." she looked at Jasmine. "Hold up you did all of that?"

"Leave it alone."

Bree shook her head. "I don't give a fuck what we did...she can't be mad about something that happened over a year ago. Y'all trying to ruin a bitches life?"

"We haven't begun to ruin your life."

"You know what, since Courtney wanna do all this, let her know when I see her, I'ma fuck her scary ass up!"

"How about you tell her yourself?" Sakura disappeared into the window and returned with a phone connected to a speaker.

"Hey girls," Courtney said from the cell. They couldn't see the screen, she was up too high, but they could hear her voice.

"Aye, dummy when I see you it's—."

"Why did you flood my show with them fucked up ass comments? And why you got niggas circling my studio?"

"I have no idea what you're talking about." Jasmine said. "But what I do know is that you took food from our mouths."

"Girl, you know that show fake anyway. Don't forget we have the audio of your cousin telling my people that your niggas taking care of you. So all that shit y'all was talking about pretty girl privilege is a fucking lie! And people deserve to know that shit!"

"You know what, so the fuck what! All y'all bitches jealous! Can't get a man to buy you a free sample let alone pay for where you sleep and what you drive and how you move. You still didn't have to send that girl into my party. I just need to make sure that recording don't go nowhere."

"So you do admit that y'all don't got no privilege."

"Yes, bitch! We kept women. So the fuck what!"

Bree touched her arm. "Maybe you shouldn't say–
–"

She yanked away from her. "Don't touch me. I don't care what these people think. I don't care about our dumbass podcast listeners either. Half of them ugly bitches couldn't get no privileges anyway."

Sakura started giggling.

"What's so funny?"

"What's funny is that you're on live right now from 'An Ugly Girls Diary' podcast. All of our listeners heard how the famous Glam Girls ain't nothing but frauds. Y'all been caught."

Jasmine felt sick.

"It looks like y'all girls can't stop running your mouth on audio."

Sure they had to start all over with a new podcast. But the plan was to use her existing base. But now after this, they weren't sure if anybody would fuck with them again.

Jasmine ran into the car crying.

But Bree hung back. "Just so you know it's not over. Get your last few winks of sleep bitch. Your days are numbered."

CHAPTER ELEVEN

A gentle rain kissed the awakening streets of Washington DC, bringing with it the sweet scent of summer. The rhythm of raindrops against rooftops merged harmoniously with the distant hum of traffic.

And Courtney's crew? They were all huddled in Plazo's apartment.

Plazo leaned against the wall with Courtney standing next to him. Sakura was sitting on the sofa and Yo-Yo was eating a bag of potato chips. Next to her was one of her baby fathers, which she nicknamed #1, since he was the first.

"She admitted to the shit she did with the food. Because of that, I believe her," Sakura said. "I know my opinion doesn't matter a lot. But I don't think they were involved with the recent stuff. Whoever been putting poop on your front door or scratching your car remains up."

"I'm just trying to think clearly."

"What's there to think about, Courtney? You heard the girl too," Plazo continued. "So what do *you* think, bae? Do you think she's responsible or not?"

"I think it's time to go to the *Mommy Moves.* Because I told y'all from the gate, if I found out, they didn't do this, they did something else. You heard what she said, Sakura. So they had this coming a long time ago."

"What about *The Liberation League*." Her brother interjected. "I don't know why you don't want to hear that, but it could be them!"

Courtney flopped on the sofa. "The last time I saw Tye, we had a serious conversation."

Her boyfriend sat next to her.

"I know this sounds weird, but I got the impression that he understood why he was locked up. I got the impression that he wanted to be punished. So I don't believe he sent them on me."

"Wow, if he's all that understanding, to take as many years as he did, maybe I should have had him as one of my baby fathers." Yo-Yo laughed.

"Don't play with me," # 1 said.

She shoved his arm. "You know, I'm playing."

"I'm serious." Courtney continued. "You gotta remember, he did everything he could to ruin me. The mother of his son. He stole from me. He took my money. He kept me away from my baby. I didn't do nothing to him he didn't deserve."

"Not to go into too much detail, but what about the shit I did to him?" Posea said. "He may forgive you, but would he really forgive me? For all we know he may be messing with you to get at me." Posea nodded.

"I just can't see it."

"Listen, them boys want him out. They been getting a lot of traction from their audience who feel like they've been done wrong by females."

Courtney was getting annoyed. "Y'all wanted me to fight. So here it is."

"Who said that?" Plazo asked.

"Well, not y'all. Adrienne." Courtney responded.

"Oh, where is she?"

"She couldn't come. Somebody has to manage the podcast. We kind of put it in syndication. Made the best of episodes. So she had to cut everything and put it together."

Plazo took a deep breath. "What I want is for you to be happy. If this is going to be it, you know I'll do what's necessary. But if it's not going to be it, Courtney, we have to move on with our lives. And if everybody said that they believe the Go-Go Girls are innocent and—"

"Glam girls," Yo-Yo corrected.

He shrugged. "Glam girls, go-go girls, who gives a fuck? But if everybody said that they innocent, and you believe them, just hit the next people, and get this done. All this shit is petty anyway. Because at the end of the day I want us gone."

"You keep saying that." Yo-Yo interjected. "What does done mean?"

"He wants me to move out of town."

"But we just got cool," Yo-Yo said concerned.

"Yeah, and I just found a friend," Sakura added.

"I'm glad he's taking her away. She's the only sister I have left," Posea said. "And I want her safe."

"We go at *Mommy Moves*." Courtney had a one-track mind. "All this other talking is dumb."

CHAPTER TWELVE

D enise from the *Mommy Moves* podcast had just pulled up at the daycare center. She was helping her two-year-old, who was more in the way than anything else, get her eight-month-old out the car seat. Just as she was walking inside, she saw a pregnant woman with a large belly moving slowly into the same building. She was crying and seemed distraught.

Denise noticed. "Hey!" She said holding her infant in one arm while gripping her two-year-old with the other. "Is everything okay?"

"Not really." She was rubbing her pregnant belly repeatedly.

"You can tell me. I won't judge you."

"It's just that I've been trying my hardest to find childcare services I can afford. And this is my fifth place. She looked at the building. "Everything is so expensive. It's almost like I have to work just to provide daycare. At this rate, there will be nothing left to pay rent."

Denise nodded. "I know the feeling. I don't know what your budget is, but this place is expensive, too. Actually it's the most expensive place because of all the amenities. 24-hour video on your baby. The best food. They teach them languages early. Everything."

The woman held her belly and sat on the ground, her back up against the daycare wall. "Wow, I might as well give up and go on welfare."

Listen, let me take my baby inside, and then I'll come back in a second."

"Why?"

"I may have something to help you."

The woman took her infant and her two-year-old into the daycare. About five minutes later, she came outside. "Sorry for keeping you waiting. Come with me and get something to eat."

The pregnant woman stood up and brushed off her butt. "Maybe you not listening to me, but I can't afford anything right now."

"Can't you see when somebody is offering you grace? Don't worry, it's on me."

Twenty minutes later, they were at a diner that served cereal and breakfast all day. Sitting in a red leather booth with silver trimming, the woman sat across from Denise.

The pregnant woman fussed with the waffle in front of her. Not really wanting the food. "I'm not trying to be rude. But you said you could help me. I really would like to know how."

"First, let me say I'm so sorry this happened to you. Being a single mother is difficult. Probably the hardest thing you've ever had to do. Is the child's father around?"

"No." She forked at her eggs. "He told me not to get pregnant for this particular reason. And what do I do? Go and get pregnant anyway. I'm such a stupid bitch." The pregnant woman was laying it on thick. "He was right per usual."

"Don't let him off that easy. If your body is able, you can have a baby whenever you're ready. He just failed because he didn't step up." Just then, Denise's phone rang. "Give me one second."

The woman shook her head while keeping her eyes on her intently.

"What's up, sis?" Denise nodded on the phone. "How many do they want?" She nodded again, and looked at the woman, and smiled. "Okay sis, I'll take care of it." Placing the phone back into her designer Chanel bag, she took a deep breath. "Sorry about that."

"No reason to be sorry. You're doing me a favor. But how can you help?"

"What if I can offer you childcare services for free?"

"Wait, what? How?"

"You have to answer the question first."

"Look at me. I'm a wreck. I would do anything for childcare services for free."

"You saying that now, but when it's time to show and prove, are you going to stay the course?"

"Not gonna lie, I don't know what you want me to do. So let me tell you what I'm not willing to do. I'm not willing to sell my body. I have a baby inside of me and I want to keep it that way. Not getting no nasty disease by letting somebody with a fetish for pregnant women dump off."

"Luckily, I would never get you to do something like that."

"At the same time my entire life is messed up right now. I'm sorry, fucked up. Let me not beat around the bush."

Denise frowned. "Earlier today you use foul language. I didn't speak on it. But, I wouldn't use that language around your baby if I were you."

"My baby's not here yet."

"But your baby is here! Your baby is with you." Her eyes were wide and wild. "And trust me when I tell you, he can hear everything you say."

And suddenly the pregnant woman was uncomfortable. "Okay, if you say so."

She glared. "I do say so. Mothers have to understand that everything they do impacts their child's lives."

The pregnant woman was getting annoyed with the preaching. "Listen, I just want daycare services. I can afford a couple hundred dollars a month. Maybe. But the prices have gone up further than that. If you can help me that's good. If not, maybe we should part ways."

"Let me just say, be glad you met me. Because I'm involved in a program for mothers just like you."

The pregnant woman leaned in and hit the record button on her phone without Denise noticing. "Go ahead."

"All you have to do is go to the bank with a check that I'll give you."

This bitch didn't waste no time. This was so good, the pregnant woman who was Sakura couldn't even stay still she was so excited. "Okay, and then what?"

"After you do that, you bring half of the money back to me and you keep the rest."

"So why don't you do it if it's so easy?"

"I have done it. I continue to do it."

"So, it's a bad check?"

"It's not a bad check. You'll see that when you get the money." She giggled. "The people who own the checks aren't from this country. And they don't want to be flagged. We're talking about immigrants. So it's their money, they just can't have access to it legally because they don't have identification. So they're willing to pay the VIG by putting a check in your name." She pointed a well-manicured finger her way.

"They trusting you with their money?"

"Of course! I've been doing this for years! Not only do they trust me, they trust *only* me. The question is, can I trust you?"

"Okay, I'm with it. How do I start?" She said, with wide eyes.

THE NEXT DAY

Sakura was in front of the bank waiting on Denise. She told her to be there at 3:00 pm and a lot of time had passed, and she was still not there.

Finally, it was in the evening, 7:00 pm to be exact and she still wasn't present. Feeling stupid, she got in her car and drove away.

"What happened again?" Courtney asked as she and Yo-Yo were looking at her. They were in Courtney's living room, hoping she will provide more answers.

Sakura cleared her throat. "I don't know why y'all keep having me repeat the story. I met with her at the diner. She told me to show up the next day, I was there and she didn't come."

"That bitch got spooked." Yo-Yo said.

Courtney sat next to her.

"To be honest I didn't know it was going to be so easy. She put me onto the scam quick."

"I'm not surprised it was easy. I heard that's what she does which is why I wanted you to go to the daycare. She gets single mothers to scam, knowing they need the money. And she acts desperate. So what happened next?"

Sakura was annoyed. "We went to the diner. After the diner, we..." Suddenly, Sakura's eyes got big.

"What?" Courtney said.

"Oh, no? Oh, no what?" Yo-Yo questioned.

"At one point, my stomach got pushed a little further down. I put it back in place under the table, but..."

"Oh my God!" Courtney stood up. "She must have seen it."

She looked up at them "I'm telling you she didn't see it. Trust me."

"How else would you explain her not showing up?"

"I think it was something else. I just don't know what."

CHAPTER THIRTEEN

As twilight descended, the city was enveloped in a humid embrace. Streetlights flickered, casting shadows that danced on buildings and homes.

Inside Courtney's cozy abode, Lawson was on the phone with a girl he had been trying to bag for the longest. She was saying all the right things, but his responses were low, so that only she could hear him. The last thing he needed was his mother walking into his room and ruining everything.

"Like I said, I'ma take you out for your birthday. Just tell your mother to drop you off at the mall. Say you're with your friend CT or something."

"You sound crazy. I don't have to lie to my mother."

He frowned. "So she just gonna let you go with a boy?"

She giggled. "My mother trust me. And like you said, it's my birthday. As long as she picks us back up where she dropped us off I'm good."

He set up on the edge of the bed. Because he didn't have the same liberties. Courtney played him close and played him close at all times. "There's one thing...my mother is gonna want to stay around."

"Stay around? For what?"

"She don't ever let me go nowhere by myself."

"Hold up, your mother treats you like a baby?"

His face reddened. It took him so long to get her and now he felt like he was about to ruin it all. He had to back out of this shit quick. "You know I'm just playing right?"

"I was about to say, boy. Because if you want to be with me you gotta be able to do stuff like this. I don't want to be worried about your mother snooping around."

He stood up and leaned against the wall. "Like I said, I can do what I want."

"Good, because I'm going to give you a kiss."

"You said that last time."

"This time—"

Suddenly the door opened, and he hung up on his girlfriend. Plazo walked inside the room and stood in the doorway. "You hungry?"

Lawson sat on the bed and looked at him. "How come you don't ever knock?"

"Because I like the element of surprise."

"Well, I don't."

"I know. That's why I do it."

Lawson giggled.

Plazo could be irritating, but he liked him because he was consistent.

"How you been though?" Plazo asked.

He shrugged. "I've been okay."

"You need anything?"

"No. Just for you to make sure you keep my mother happy."

Plazo smiled. Very impressed with his response. "Now you gonna tell me about my woman?"

"I'm serious."

Plazo respected the young man, so he wanted to keep it real. "I'm gonna keep your mother happy. But in keeping her happy, I'm also going to be considering you too. And you may not like my plans, but understand as always, it's to keep you safe."

"What does that mean?"

"Now you really in my business."

"It's just that—"

"You got a girlfriend." Plazo interrupted.

"How you know?"

"I was your age before. I see all the signs." He looked at the phone tucked under the pillow. "What's she like?"

"She real pretty. And she treats me nice."

"That's good. If she treats you right, you're making the right decision already young man."

"I am, which is why I don't want us to move again." He begged with his eyes.

Plazo walked closer. "Whether we move again or not, know that your mother is going to always put you first."

"So if she's going to put me first, then tell her I don't want to go."

He smiled. "I'm gonna order some pizza. You want some?"

"You know I want some."

Plazo chuckled, tapped the wall, and walked out.

Courtney entered only to see her fine ass man sitting in the living room watching TV, the lights out. Where she left him. Kicking off her shoes one by one, she walked toward him. He positioned the pillows the way she liked, and she eased on to the sofa, tucked her feet up under her body and rested on him. He put his arm around her and pulled her closer. Immediately she felt at home.

"He had pizza. Damn near half a box. He's been out ever since."

She laughed. "I'm so happy you're here."

"Did it work out?"

"No." She nestled closer.

He sighed deeply. "What's the plan?"

"I really don't know. Like I don't believe it's *The Liberation League* and I don't even have closure on *Mommy Moves*."

"You want to give me the details? So we can work it out together. Maybe I can help you see an angle you didn't see before."

She raised her head and looked up at him before resting it down again. "Can we do it tomorrow? Right now all I want is to be up under you."

"You sure that's all you want to do?" He smiled.

"You won't even let me get cleaned up?"

"I'm waiting on an answer."

She sat up straight and straddled him. "I'm ready to do whatever you want to do."

He picked her up and carried her toward the room. "Then fuck you waiting on?"

Dear Diary,

I'm scared now.

I was 100 percent sure that we would be able to hit the Mommy Moves. But maybe I did make a mistake. Maybe I'm going too far, but nothing in me wants to quit.

I'm tired of being afraid and I'm tired of being a pushover. I'm tired of having to pack my son up to start all over in a different place.

That's what I'm telling myself.

But it feels like something bad is about to happen. Something I'm not prepared for.

For now, a least I have Plazo.

At least I have Lawson.

At least I have people around me who are willing to fight for me.

That counts for something, right?

CHAPTER FOURTEEN

The early morning fog clung to the streets of Washington DC, shrouding the city in a mysterious veil. The faint glow of the rising sun struggled against what looked like white smoke, casting a surreal light over the sleepy streets.

Courtney was inside of her temporary studio doing her best to stay focused. They rented two offices in a building where therapists met their clients. And although she knew she had to host her podcast, which meant entertaining, her mind was elsewhere.

"Are you okay?" Adrienne asked.

"Why you keep asking me that?" She said as she put on her headset.

"Because I need you to focus. We're about to go on air. And I can tell before you even open your mouth that you aren't here for real."

"I'll be good. I just have to—." Suddenly, Courtney's phone rang. When she removed it from her purse, she saw it was Sakura. Quickly she took off the headset. "I have to take this."

Adrienne rolled her eyes. "Of course you do."

Standing up, she took the phone call. "What is it? I'm about to go on air."

"She called me."

"Who?"

"Denise." Her eyes widened. "Where are you?"

"I'm at the studio, come right away."

"Give me the address and I'll be in route."

"You're spending an awful lot of time with that loser. Think about it, she shows up from nowhere and you just happen to rescue her? People want to see you out of position. Why are you giving her an easy way?"

"I don't believe she is out to get me. She's genuine."

"You keep saying that but if you aren't smart, watch what happens next."

"What does that supposed to mean?"

Fifteen minutes later, Sakura walked inside. Since her mind was already preoccupied, she told Adrienne to run some more *best of* episodes which she was sure would annoy her fan base. But, Courtney was fine with it because she knew she would make it up to them later.

Standing inside of one of the offices, Sakura was breathing heavily. Despite running inside, she could see the excitement all in her eyes.

"Okay I need you to calm down and without missing a beat, tell me what happened."

"She apologized for not meeting with me. Said she had to pick up her child. Said the baby got sick. I'm just happy she got back."

Suddenly Adrienne walked into the room. "And you're here because?"

Sakura looked at her with the lower gaze. "I'm here because I don't want to do anything without making sure it's cool with Courtney."

"Well, you could have said that shit over the phone."

"I'm sorry but do you have a problem with me or something?"

"You know what actually, I do. We have a podcast to run. And you interrupted for something that you could have texted about."

"Not really." Courtney interjected. "But I hear you though. Is there a reason why you came into this office?"

"Yeah, I have to grab some things from the closet."

"Well, I'm gonna leave you at it." She focused back on Sakura. "Come with me."

When the door was closed, Courtney said, "What else did she say?"

"That was it. Like I said, I just wanted to make sure it was cool with you, because I don't want to do anything if it's not."

"This is what we wanted," Courtney nodded. "This is...this was a part of the plan. But my instincts are telling me something is going on."

"Ok now you're confusing me."

"Don't go."

Her eyebrows rose. "What? Why?"

"I don't trust it."

"Courtney, if you're going to get back at them, I need more information to get the bitch arrested. Them little bitty recordings I have is nothing. We need more. Plus in the state of Maryland, you can't even record somebody unless both people agree. I think it's the same in DC too."

"Technically, if she's scamming, we have enough to watch her from afar. To get some video recording instead. Something we could run on the show by showing everybody."

"But I thought you didn't do visuals."

"Not of myself, but I always host video if it's available about a subject. It's just that my thing has never been the police."

"I don't like the police either. But I like it for her. And you did the streaming thing with the *Glam Girls*! I thought this time you wanted to go deeper."

"I do, but I'll say it again, don't go."

"Courtney, I think this a bad mistake. Like I really want you to get your revenge. I can tell this is on your mind heavily."

"You just met me. Are you sure it's not about you?"

"So because I just met you, I don't care?"

"I never said that."

"Okay, well if you didn't say that, then you know that this has to be done. I can handle it."

"I get all that. But, I'm saying no. If I decide to change my mind, we'll do that." She placed a hand on her shoulder. "Trust me, she's not going anywhere."

"Are you scared?"

"For the people I care about? You included. Yes. Let it go."

"Okay." She turned to leave out. "Oh, and I don't trust your friend."

"Who? Yo-Yo?"

"No, I fuck with Yo-Yo! Hard! I'm talking about that engineer girl. She gives me the creeps."

"Listen at you...coming from nowhere trying to tell me about my people." She started laughing until she realized she was laughing alone. "Why do you say that?"

"I know I'm young, but I know snakes when I see 'em. And you have one in your midst." She gave her a hug. "I'll wait for your word, but if I were you, I would look into that girl." She walked out.

CHAPTER FIFTEEN

The city of Washington DC lay draped in a muggy blanket as twilight deepened into a sexy ass May night. The air, thick with humidity, carried the vibrant rhythms of passing cars, blending with the distant laughter of night watchers. Streetlights cast a hazy glow on the damp pavements, reflecting in the occasional puddle from an earlier rain.

But outside they could do whatever the fuck they wanted. Because one street lover was taken care of business in the bedroom. Yo-Yo was riding Baby father #3's dick and she loved being on top of him because when they were together, he moved inside of her like a clock.

Left, down, right, up.

Left, down, right, up.

Left, down, right, up.

Quicker...quicker...quicker.

He had the code.

He knew how to please her and he made it his business to hit the right spots each time. And when she asked him what exactly he did to make her feel so good, he said, "I'm not telling you just so you could tell #1 and 2."

She giggled because he was right.

Before long, like in the past, he busted inside of her. Her entire body trembled. And she took him in fully. She may have lived in the projects but to her, she was living the good life. She felt safe and wanted. More than anything, she felt loved by the people in her circle.

After she got off of him, she cleaned up and threw on some sweatpants and a jacket. "What you want to eat?"

"I don't know. The Jerk Off open?" He chuckled. "If so, get me some jerk chicken and oxtails. Rice and peas. And make sure the cocoa bread is fresh."

"Like I would ever let them give you something that's not right." She shook her head. "The boys are in their rooms. Just keep an eye on them."

"I'm watching all my niggas."

Leaving the room, she walked into the living room where Baby father #1 and #2 were playing a video game. "I'm getting food from the Jerk Off. What y'all want?"

"Whatever he got." #1 said still glued onto the game.

"Same." #2 responded.

They would have offered to go but knew she would say no. Yo-Yo liked being in the streets. She liked fresh air whenever possible and that meant getting out of the projects from time to time, even if it was for a food run.

Sliding into her Jeep she played her favorite music. As she drove, she thought about the future she was building for her sons. And all the things she wanted in their lives. At the current moment, she had over $260,000 saved up. She didn't know what her boys wanted to do with their lives. But if they wanted to go to vocational school or college, she and their fathers were going to fund it fully.

More than anything, she had plans to get a little house in the county, where her babies wouldn't have to worry about bullets, boundaries, or bodies. Because although it didn't bother her when it came to her sons, it was like a nightmare.

Pulling up to the Jerk Off, a Caribbean restaurant, she parked her car. "What up, Yo-Yo?" Someone yelled outside.

"What it do, baby!" She responded.

Every time she moved, someone would wave at her. They had better speak. They recognized a real bitch when they saw one.

Opening the restaurant door, the cashier said, "Hey, there."

"Hey, friend."

"How many boxes you gonna need for that football team you got over there? Four or five?"

Yo-Yo shook her head. "Not a football team yet. But if my niggas have anything to do with it, it'll be that way soon. Plus, don't act like you know me."

She laughed. "Girl, the way you eat, if I don't know you, who else do?"

"I'm messing with you. But to answer your question seven boxes."

They both broke out into laughter.

Yo-Yo gave her the order, which totaled up to over $200 worth of food. "I'm gonna go to the bathroom."

"Do what you gotta do, baby."

Yo-Yo pissed and washed her hands. Checking herself in the mirror, she liked what she saw when she realized every nameplate and chain was in its proper position. Washing her hands again, she walked outside and up to the window.

But the cashier seemed different. "What's up with the food?"

"You said you wanted the fried chicken box, right?"

Yo-Yo frowned. Because that was nowhere near what she ordered. Every man in her household wanted jerk chicken. Because they cooked it that good. But she wasn't dumb either.

She looked behind her, and then back at the cashier. There were a few people in there she didn't recognize, but she couldn't call it. "Yeah, the fried chicken box."

"Well, I don't got time to be frying the wrong parts. So come on back here and tell me which parts you do want. Last time you complained and gave me a bad review."

"Well I ain't want to do it to you, but the food was fucked up." Yo-Yo's heartbeat kicked up heavily. She never in her life gave Marisa a bad review. She knew even more that something was off. "You know I always been for real about my food."

Walking back into the kitchen, the moment the door closed, Marisa said, "I need you to get the fuck out of here." She was so close. She could smell the soda from her breath. "My brother gonna take you home."

Yo-Yo look past her and saw her brother. Stacker. A big dude with dreads down his back.

Yo-Yo nodded. "What's wrong though?"

"Some girls came in here with Roberto and Victor. And not for nothing but I think they mean to do you harm."

Roberto and Victor sounded familiar although she couldn't call it. "How you figure?"

"Because I know for a fact nair one of them hoes like Caribbean food. My brother said that the moment they walked in, their eyes were wild and crazy. And they kept looking in the direction you walked into. It really started coming in line when Roberto seemed interested in what he called the *Redbone with acne scars*. But we told them niggas you weren't here. But they may be back."

"That's me all right."

"You telling me."

Marisa nodded to her brother. Before Yo-Yo left, she turned around to the woman, "I appreciate this shit right here! For real!"

"I know you do. You just make sure nothing fucking happens to you! I would go off. Also know that this right here, will always be a safe haven."

They hugged quickly and let go.

Her brother rushed Yo-Yo out the back door and to the car. As they drove down the street, she knew exactly where she heard the names from now.

How could she be so stupid?

She heard them from Jasmine's cousin.

Fuck!

They were all at Courtney's house. Posea, Plazo, Sakura, Yo-Yo, and even Adrienne.

"It was the Glam Girls." Courtney said.

"I know that now. I'm just trying to figure out how they found me."

"Damn!" Plazo said, "I'm just glad them people at the restaurant were 100. This shit could have gone a whole different way."

"You telling me," Yo-Yo said.

Posea shook his head. "Alright, I'm gonna get the rest of the family together and—"

"No!" Yo-Yo stopped him. "No war yet."

"No war yet? They tried to—"

"We don't know what they tried to do. You remember the last time we called the war. Lot of people lost real men who got caught up for no reason. If it'll be that it'll be that. At the end of the day

By T. STYLES

whatever they tried, didn't go down. They failed. Let's just play it easy. For now."

"Well, I'm taking you to get your truck," Posea said.

"Baby father #1 already grabbed it. It's at the crib now."

Courtney stood up. "Shit getting thick."

"Ain't it? Plus the girl, Denise called again. That makes it two times since I last told you," Sakura said, "And I really think we should meet her. Especially if you're about to bounce. You don't want no loose ends. At the end of the day shit already hot. So let it get hotter."

"I can always go with her." Yo-Yo said. "To watch her back unless you want to."

"My sister don't show her face. Never has and never will."

Courtney felt low. Although she knew that was not her brother's intent. He was speaking facts. But it didn't make her feel any better. "It's not that. I just know that the moment they see me, they would know what's up."

"But nobody has ever seen your face." Adrienne added.

"They have though."

"And even if they didn't, we got this," Yo-Yo responded, rolling her eyes at Adrienne.

Sakura caught it. And realized Yo-Yo didn't fuck with her either.

"So just leave it. It was a bad suggestion on my part," Yo-Yo said. "It's me and Sakura. Plus after all that just happened, I need some action."

"Me too." Sakura responded.

"But I'm watching y'all's back." Posea said.

"So what you think, Courtney? We gonna do it?" Sakura questioned.

Courtney thought a little...long and hard. "Let it be done." Courtney moved closer. "I just need everybody safe. And you gotta report to me the moment this shit over. Don't have me waiting all day."

"We got you. Trust me," Yo-Yo nodded.

Then Lawson came out his room. "Hey little cuz." Yo-Yo said. "It's nice to finally meet you."

"Lawson, this is your cousin Yo-Yo," Courtney said.

"I got a son your age. He would love to hang with–_"

"Let's stay focused," Courtney interjected, cutting her off.

Lawson wasn't having any of it. If he had more family he wanted to meet them and his mother was blocking. "How come I can't meet my cousins?"

"Just leave it alone!" Courtney yelled.

"But—"

"Lawson, you heard your mother." Plazo said. "Go to your room."

He stormed away, slamming the door behind him.

"I could bring him over here you know." Yo-Yo said. "That way he could meet—"

"Damn, how come y'all don't respect boundaries!" Adrienne said. "The woman made it clear she don't want her son out in the streets. So leave it at that."

"If you wanna have a private conversation with me about your problem, I'm with that shit." Yo-Yo said. "But never interrupt me when I'm talking to family again. That's your final warning from me."

She shrugged. "It can be whatever."

Sakura smiled.

"Y'all cut all this shit out!" Courtney said. "The last thing we need to be is beefing with each other. Let's hold it together!"

Yo-Yo and Sakura heard Courtney but they were also staring Adrienne down.

CHAPTER SIXTEEN

U nder a moonlit sky, Washington DC rested in a rare moment of serene beauty. The buzz of the day had faded into a gentle hum of nightlife, as the moon cast a soft silver glow over the diner.

Sakura, very impatient, waited in the same spot she met Denise in before. It was something about diners that they all loved. Courtney had her favorite diner, and it appeared that Denise had hers too.

Ready for whatever, unlike in the past, this time Sakura had eyes watching her. Yo-Yo was in the corner with a bad wig to hide her identity and Posea was on the other end with a cap pulled way down over his eyes.

A few seconds later, Denise walked inside. She was carrying her baby but wore a cheerful smile on her face. Sitting in front of her, she said, "I want to apologize."

"Apologize for what?"

"For how I handled you. I should have gotten back with you earlier."

"Like I told you before, I'm not even worried about that." She rubbed her fake belly. "I'm just grateful for the opportunity."

"I would have been here on time with the check, but I have a podcast to run."

"You have a podcast?" She questioned as if she didn't already know.

"Yep. Been doing it for fifteen years. It's for mothers. Helping them navigate the world like I'm trying to do with you."

Sakura was done hearing all of the madness. She wanted to get onto business. So badly her leg shook rapidly under the table. "So where's the check?"

Denise looked around and dug into her soft pink baby's bag. Pulling out the check, she slid it across the table. "That's your name on the fake ID, right?"

Her eyes were as wide as saucers. "Yep, that's it."

"Okay, so all you have to do is what I told you. Go into the bank. Give them your ID and the check, cash it, and I'll be outside waiting to get my portion."

"And after I do this, I'm able to get free childcare? That seems like a lot."

"I didn't want to tell you this before because I didn't know if I could trust you. But seeing as how you handled me not being there, well, I figure you're a real one."

"Of course I am." She cleared her throat.

"That daycare center belongs to me and my sister."

She felt that was weird, but whatever. "Why didn't you tell me that?"

"Because I didn't want you begging for free childcare if I couldn't trust you. But now that I know I can, I want to be able to put you in a better position. A lot of the women I help have their children there. They also have homes and cars. Like, I'm really taking care of people's babies."

The bragging was gross, but she let her have it. "Wow!"

"There are children in there who have special needs and can't even begin to help themselves. Childcare for those babies are doubled. So I'm doing a lot."

Sakura nodded, "God will bless your little old soul." She winked. "Okay. I'm going to do what you want and I won't let you down. I'll cash it tomorrow. Which bank?"

She slid another piece of paper. "Go to this one. Go to the third teller. I don't care how long you have to wait. Don't go to anyone but the third teller. A black girl. With red, wild hair. You'll know her when you see her."

Sakura reached across the table and shook her hand.

When Denise was long gone, Sakura rushed outside and got into Courtney's car. She told her everything about the girl owning the daycare and about the bank. She even played a portion of the audio recording so she could get a real feel of the scheme she was running. And after all of that, Courtney immediately said, "We have to let this one go."

"What? Why? We got her dead to rights!" She was very angry.

"She said she's taking care of people with special needs, Sakura. What I look like stealing their livelihoods away? I'll get at her another way."

"I feel like you're being afraid when you don't have to. Nobody told her to be in charge of the babies of the world. All I know is, she's doing shit illegally, and she should pay!"

"Leave it alone. I'm not fucking around."

"But I can't stand that bitch."

"Why you that mad, Sakura? Help me understand."

She looked away. "There's just something about her I don't like."

"Well, that's not enough. Because I need to know right now are you doing this for me or yourself?"

"You!"

"Ok, I'm telling you I don't want you involved. I'm telling you to leave it alone. So if you doing it for me, it stops right here."

"Alright. I'ma let it go."

"Good, now, give me a hug."

"Nah...I'm good. I feel like I'm coming down with something. And I don't wanna get you sick."

She got out the car.

Driving home, Sakura thought about the situation. She didn't like Denise for a lot of reasons, but the main reason she didn't like her was because she knew her. Her baby's father, her first love, was stolen by her.

She was surprised Denise didn't recognize her face. After all, Denise told him to leave her. That she didn't have a future. And watched from the car when he broke her heart only for her to fall on the ground crying.

It was amazing how people hurt others and never saw revenge coming. That was one of the reasons she knew who Courtney was. She was a legend. Her legend. And now a personal friend. And because of it, she would ride for her to death. Even if it was against her will.

Envious and still bitter over losing her first love, Sakura went to the bank, just like Denise told her in the hopes Courtney would take the evidence which would cause Denise to get locked up. She was even recording.

The moment she walked inside, she saw the woman with the red hair, but the teller to the right was finishing up her customer. And so she let the person behind her go first. She had to do that three more times before finally the woman was ready to take her.

When it was her time, she walked up to her, looked around and slid the check over. "I'm with Denise."

She frowned. "Who is Denise?"

She realized at that moment Denise didn't tell her to give her name so she never should have brought it up in the first place. She hadn't been there for five minutes and already she was fucking up.

"Uh, nobody. But here's my identification."

She took the identification and read the check. Looking at it with closer eyes, she squinted a bit. She looked at Sakura and back at the check.

"Everything cool?"

The woman smiled. "Yes, of course."

She took the check in the back for what seemed like forever. Finally, the woman returned with an envelope filled with money. "I gave it to you in hundreds since it's $2,000. Did you want it in lower denominations?"

She could've used smaller bills, but at this point Sakura just wanted to take the cash and bounce. So she said, "No, uh...just give me the money."

The moment the envelope slid across the counter, the doors from the bank opened and the police entered. They grabbed Sakura from the back and handled her roughly. Her face was planted on the cold floor, and she saw so many black boots she didn't know which officer had their hands on her body.

She wanted to faint.

One of the cops pulled her back to her feet. Now in cuffs, she wobbled a little.

"What's...what's going on? I didn't do anything!"

"Of course you didn't." The police officer said. "That's why you using a stolen check."

"Somebody gave me that check. I was trying to solve a case."

"What are you talking about?" The teller said. "That's my name on the check."

"You heard that? So why do you have a check written from this young lady right here? After her house was broken into just a week prior. And then to add insult to injury you come where she works! What kind of person are you?"

Sakura felt weak.

She had been set up. If only she listened to Courtney. The thing was, she didn't. And none of it mattered now.

Courtney was at home cooking spaghetti and meatballs for the men in her life when the phone rang. Wiping her hand on her towel she answered.

"You have a collect call from DC Jail to accept—"

She accepted the call and sat down.

"Hello...hello...Courtney, it's me!"

"Sakura!" She rose to her feet. "What happened?"

Silence.

She knew immediately. "Please say you didn't." Her entire body trembled.

"Don't talk, Courtney. I just...I just wanted to say I'm sorry. That you are an awesome friend. And if I did anything to ruin it, I'll hate myself forever."

"But what happened?"

"Please don't talk. I don't want you to get in this at all." She cried, doing her best to protect her. "I just wanted you to know that you're the coolest person I've met in a long time. Bye."

Courtney and Yo-Yo were on the speakerphone inside Courtney's bedroom. Denise had successfully put a hole into her plans. Taking Sakura hurt on more than one level. She cared about the girl. She literally became her friend.

"I'm glad you decided to take my call," Denise laughed.

"Why did you do it?"

"You mean why did I stop you from getting me before I got you? You mean why did I stop you from ruining my business like you did the Glam Girls?"

Courtney and Yo-Yo looked at one another.

"Let's just say you've made some enemies. Enemies amongst your peers. And let's just say they have your friend's phone. Let's also say they made call after call and became aware of your plan. I owe them girls, my life."

Courtney felt sick. The fact that Sakura was in jail bothered her greatly. And she couldn't help but feel like it was her fault. "She wasn't going to fuck with you."

"Let me make this clear. I wasn't trying to take out your podcast. Whoever after you is not me. So, I would be well within my rights to tell you the truth based on what you tried to pull. So I didn't have people come to your studio. I didn't spam your comment section. And all the other wild shit you think I did." She paused. "Stay out of my way and I'll stay out of yours. Goodbye."

Dropping the phone on the bed, Courtney flopped down.

Yo-Yo dragged a hand down her face. "I got people in the jail. They already watching our girl."

"I told her to leave it alone. Why the fuck didn't she listen?! I knew something was off!" She said it multiple times.

"If you told her and she did it anyway that's on her. Not you."

"Then why does it hurt so bad?"

CHAPTER SEVENTEEN

August 15th

Denise was still on her game after putting Courtney in her place. And now, she didn't feel like she had any trouble in the world.

The moment she got home from the diner, when she first met Sakura, she found out from a friend who knew Bree and Jasmine that Courtney was on some slick shit. Luckily Jasmine snapped a picture of Sakura hanging out of the window, and they told all of the friends in the podcasting world to be careful if they saw that bitch.

So she did.

Outside of that, things were looking up for Denise. Her daycare center was more popular than ever and she was able to get more children. Many who were able to get into prestigious schools for first grade. Not to mention her podcast, *Mommy Moves*, was a staple for single mothers.

But she wanted more. In her mind, she wanted the women to take motherhood seriously from the day of inception all the way until their child was twenty-one-years old. That meant eating healthy and even having limited stress.

So what she was a scammer. Her listeners weren't aware of it.

She provided them with firm advice to better their lives to hear her tell it. Things they could actually use to become better parents. And to save a little money. And to think, a few months ago Courtney was about to ruin it all.

Had Bree and Jazz not told her about what was coming her way, she would have been caught red handed.

Now in her daycare, they were getting things together for the August birthday parties. August was always a big month for celebration at her center. She and her sister spent hours once a year trying to figure out why the majority of the children seemed to have birthdays in that month. She never got a good reason so she let it go.

"Okay, everything is set on my end. The break room is really nice." Ebony said.

"Good, some of the parents are going to help because you and I both know how crazy it gets in here with these kids. All high on candy and sugar."

"What we need to be doing is hiring more people."

Denise waved the air. "And we'll do all of that, just not right now. It's too much to juggle to get a larger staff. Plus do we really want people around here asking questions?"

She gave her a gaze to remind her that part of their income came from the scams. Not necessarily just checks. They were big on credit cards too.

"You're right."

"We need to keep this in house. For now."

"Exactly."

As they continued to get the party together, suddenly, an officer walked inside. "Is Denise Kelly here?"

Denise frowned and looked at her sister before focusing back on the cops. "Yes."

"Good. This is what's going to happen. You are going to come with me, and then we're going to come inside and take the children out to the vans. When the children are out in the vans, we are going to take you to the precinct and formally book you."

Denise held her stomach as if she were pregnant. "Book me? For what?"

"I'm not going to get into detail about that right now. Just know that I have a warrant." He rose the document in the air. And then set it on the table.

"What I need to make sure is that you understand what I'm saying."

"I do understand, but I don't know why you doing this. One of the parents complain?"

"I don't have to tell you why. You're not listening. If you really care about these children though, you will come quietly."

Denise felt ill.

"Is it another adult here?"

"Yes, my sister." She placed her hand over her heart.

The officer grabbed her by her arm and quietly walked her outside.

A second later, three women entered the daycare center and spoke quietly to the children. Most were upset about not being able to participate in the party, but for the most part, every child was safely put in the van, leaving her sister, Ebony, alone.

She walked up to them, hoping to get more information. "Can you tell me why this is going on?"

"It's all in the warrant. And I'm sure your sister will tell you more when she makes her first call." One of the social workers said. "In the meantime, this center will be closed down. If I were you, I would make preparations to find another job."

Denise was charged with check and credit card fraud. Turns out there was an open case on her that she was unaware of, that was triggered when Sakura was locked up. While Denise was successful at getting Sakura arrested, what she didn't realize was that when she handed her the check, both Posea and Yo-Yo were at the diner.

They didn't even remember that they had the footage until months later. When it was revealed that whoever stole the checks from the cashier had also broken into her home, they started doing a little more work. That's when the case file that was already pending was reopened, and she was finally convicted.

Courtney never wanted to get the police involved. But Denise made her change her mind.

Sitting in her cell, Denise was wiping her eyes after crying all day, something she had done daily when Sakura walked inside. Thinking she wanted to fight, Denise jumped up. "What you...what you doing in my cell?"

"I'll tell you that, but you should know you don't have anything you own in here. So the cell you're claiming is not yours. That luxury lifestyle is a thing of the past. Besides, I have a message for you."

"I don't want anything from you."

"Is that right? Because, you seemed to want everything from me before. When you framed me for this shit."

Denise glared. "You tried to come at me. All I was trying to do was protect myself."

Sakura waved the air. "Denise, it don't even matter for real. I had no business going to the bank. But somebody we both know wanted me to tell you, you should've never fucked with her."

"Maybe I did do it. That whore had it coming. All the shit she did to people. I hope they catch her soon." She laughed.

Later that day, Sakura got on the phone and called Courtney.

"Do you need anything? Are they treating you ok in there?"

"I'm fine. You've taken care of me enough. I have more money in here than I had when I was home."

"I'm just sorry you got caught up with all this."

"Listen, Denise said maybe she did do it. It looked like we were right all along." She grinned. "At least she in here with me. I knew I was right!"

"Are you sure you're not just saying that because you still don't like her?"

Silence.

"Sakura?"

"I'm telling you what she said. But I have been wrong."

CHAPTER EIGHTEEN

Dear Diary,

The last few months have been up and down, but I'm so happy that finally I get the life that I have been wanting.

Somebody who knows Denise called and said that she was responsible for sending people down the studio. And that she was responsible for flooding my timeline, and the broken windows and everything else. Yes the person was in jail, but they had details I felt only the perpetrator should know.

Who knows?

But now, months later, everything seemed to flow. I got a good man. My son is thriving in school. My relationship with my brother is closer than ever. And I'm even getting along with Yo-Yo.

The only thing that makes me feel a kind of way is that Sakura is still locked up. But the way she's handling it is wild. It's almost like she wanted to punish herself. Like she blamed herself for going to get the check. And she'll be out in a year so everything is cool.

By T. STYLES

The guilt she had before she even met me was probably why I found her drunk that morning.

And come to think of it, I never asked her what she was doing out there. I had my own stuff going on.

All I can say, diary is that things are going in my favor.

And there is absolutely nothing to be worried about.

CHAPTER NINETEEN
NOVEMBER 6TH

A s the sun set on a chilly evening, the city's lights twinkled to life, casting a warm glow against the brisk air. The sound of crunching leaves underfoot mixed with the distant murmur of traffic found it like music. Wrapped in thick coats, people hurried along the sidewalks, their breath visible in the cool air.

It was a cold fucking day.

Courtney and Adrienne had just finished another *'An Ugly Girl's Diary'* episode. It was their fifth season, and they felt they ended it with a bang.

But Adrienne had been acting differently lately. Even though months had passed since the first comments flooded the podcast line, she never was her usual cheerful self. Normally they both would be sad and complaining about something so Courtney never noticed dips in her mood. But Courtney had a lot of things to look forward to. So she felt Adrienne's negativity every minute they spent together.

It was like Adrienne was preparing to make an exit, and every day for months, Courtney was waiting for her to do just that.

By T. STYLES

"Can we talk?" Adrienne said.

Here it comes.

"What is it?" She was sitting behind her desk and pushed everything to the side.

"I wanna say that working with you and being on this podcast has been one of the best things to ever have happened to me. Like for real. I never saw this as part of my world and to know that it's possible because of you. I just don't know what to say."

Courtney walked up to her and held her tightly. "I don't know what's gotten into you, but you don't have to thank me. We helped each other."

"I get it. I just want you to know where I'm coming from, that's all."

"Is there anything else?"

"Not really."

"Well, I gotta get out of here, girl. I got a man and a son at home. And Lawson has been feeling pretty bad lately."

"What you mean?"

"He's coming down with something. I just hope he doesn't give it to me."

Adrienne frowned. "He's out of school?"

"Yeah, for a couple of days."

"Well let me know when he goes back. That's the one thing I can't stand about kids. They always bringing something else home from school. Instead of just they homework."

"Well I'll talk to you later."

"Later! Good show too!"

Courtney winked at her and walked toward the door, grabbing her coat and purse.

When she pushed the door open, she was shocked to see Tye Gates, her son's father leaning against a truck.

Her heartbeat rapidly.

He was looking down at his phone so he didn't see her come out, but she saw him.

What the fuck was he doing there?

She rushed back inside and locked the door. Dropping her purse and coat, she quickly walked up to Adrienne. "He's here."

"Who?"

"Tye Gates."

She glared. "Wait! He's out of prison?"

"I gotta make a call. I gotta call...." She ran back and got her phone and brought it back into the office where Adrienne was. She was so nervous she didn't know who to call.

By T. STYLES

"Who are you about to hit?"

"I gotta call my brother. And then I have to call my man."

While Courtney dialed the number Adrienne said, "Why would Tye be here? Why wouldn't he just go home? Been out only a minute and he's here already!"

Courtney made her calls and within seconds, both her brother and her man were there. Since he couldn't be left home alone, Lawson was also in the back seat, but they parked far enough away so that Tye wouldn't see them. The only reason why Lawson was there was because Courtney didn't trust anybody with him except her brother or Plazo.

When she went back outside, she was relieved when she only saw her brother and boyfriend.

Tye was gone.

Later on that day, they were in Courtney's house. Posea, Yo-Yo, and Plazo all worrying about Tye. Lawson was in his room coughing. And to make matters worse, Courtney felt ill too. But there was no time to be sick.

"How did he know where you worked?" Posea asked, holding his jaw due to a tooth that was driving him mad.

"I have no idea." She grabbed a tissue from the dispenser off the living room table.

"This nigga gonna get out of jail and come see you?" Plazo added. "What is wrong with this dude? I'm confused."

"It gets worse. He hit my phone. At work."

"Why didn't you tell me?" Plazo asked.

"I was waiting for you guys to come. And I lost track. Everything happened so fast. Anyway, he talking about he wanna see his son. When I never agreed to no shit like that."

Posea pulled himself together. "I'm gonna ask around. Find out how long he's been out and what he wants from you. But I don't want you to worry."

"It's too late for that."

He hugged her, dapped Plazo and walked out the door.

Plazo strolled up to her and massaged her shoulders before kissing her gently. "I don't want you worried. I'm here. I'm not going back to my crib until

I know without a doubt that you and Lawson are okay.
It's going to work out. Trust me."

CHAPTER TWENTY

A few days later, as the first light of dawn broke over Washington DC, a crisp November morning unfolded. The city awoke to a symphony of muted sounds. The distant rumble of early-morning traffic, the soft rustling of autumn leaves in the gentle breeze, and the faint chirping of birds greeting the new day.

None of that shit mattered to Courtney.

Because whatever Lawson had, he definitely gave it to her. She was feeling under the weather, a nagging cough and a headache clouding her morning as she dropped her son off at school. It didn't help matters that Lawson had questions.

Like, who was Tye Gates? Was he his father? Would she let him meet him? Questions that as far as Courtney was concerned, didn't matter. She was mommy and daddy.

As she approached the school, she looked over at him. "Are you sure you're okay?"

"Ma, I feel better. Plus I want to get out the house. And the past couple of days you've been sad."

"I haven't been sad, Lawson. Anyway, I just want to make sure you're not still sick and giving it to everybody else at school. I'm going to trust you, but if you feel bad, let me know, and I'll come get you." She coughed a few times.

"Okay, ma. Dang, let it go."

When Lawson exited the car, she got out rushed over to him and hugged him. Usually he would fight back, but knowing she needed this more than he did, he let it slide.

When she let him go, she watched as he disappeared into his high school. But the moment she turned around, before she could enter her car, she was facing Ebony, Denise's sister.

Looking like a mad woman, Ebony had her arms crossed over her chest.

Courtney coughed a few times. The cold air, attacking her body. "Not today."

She moved to the right, but Ebony blocked her. She moved to the left in the same direction.

"What is your problem?"

"My sister is still locked up."

"Well, if you do the crime you should do the time. But what that got to do with me though? And why the fuck are you at my son's school?"

"We were helping a lot of people! And you ruined it!"

"If you're talking about children with special needs, I found out that was a lie. Your sister doesn't do anything for anybody but herself. Using those single mothers because she know they needed it! So bitch get out my face."

Before Courtney could walk away, a sharp pain exploded in her belly. Prior to that moment, she just suffered a fever and a light cough.

But what was this pain?

When she looked down, she saw thick burgundy fluid spilling onto the ground and dampening the concrete beneath her feet. And she knew exactly what was going on. "You...You just stabbed me."

Slowly she looked at Ebony, whose face was twisted in rage. It was obvious she didn't care. And it was obvious if she could help it, she would do it again.

"You should have stayed out of our lives. You've taken everything from us. And I hope you die bitch."

Ebony ran away, and Courtney collapsed on the ground.

When Courtney woke up, she was in a hospital bed. The smell of medicine and disinfectant in the air. Her boyfriend, Plazo, was right beside her. He was worried, but relieved that she was alive.

"How long have I been here?" She asked. Her throat dry.

He gripped her hand and held it closely. "How are you baby? You've been here for 48 hours."

"It seem like it happened from nowhere."

"What's all this about now?"

"It was Ebony. Denise's sister."

"Denise's sister? I thought everything was good."

"Where is Lawson?"

"Lawson's still at school. I'll scoop him when I leave. Oh...you definitely got the flu. The doctors checked."

"So I'm stabbed and I'm sick."

The room felt heavy. The reality of her situation sinking in. This wasn't about her anymore. If somebody was willing to stab her at her child's school, how could she be sure they wouldn't do the same to Lawson?

Their conversation was suddenly interrupted by the arrival of Tye. His entrance was steady and his steps assured.

When Plazo saw his girls face, he knew exactly who he was. Not to mention he resembled Lawson. "What the hell you doing here, nigga? You crazy?"

"I heard about what happened."

"We don't have no relationship, Tye." Courtney said. "Even if we did, your son is not here. So why are you at the hospital?"

"Because I needed to make sure you were okay. You are the mother of my son. And I'm trying to talk to you like adults. Leave the past behind. Why won't you let me?"

"Because I want you to leave me the fuck alone. I warned you what would happen if you reached out when you were arrested. Are you really willing to risk it all?"

"Yes. For a relationship with my son I am. I want to meet Lawson. And be the father I didn't have."

Her eyebrows rose. "How you know his name?"

Silence.

Plazo, not being able to take more of it, rose and shoved him across the room. His body slammed into a chair, but he got up on his feet quickly. Before they knew it, they were in a full-blown fist fight. Left swing, right swing, left swing, right swing. It was so violent that the staff members outside rushed to get security. This was the last thing she needed.

After hearing many footsteps coming in their direction, Tye ran away. The room was suddenly filled with police officers and staff members asking a bunch of questions. With everything they had going on in the streets this was not a good look. Courtney was too weak to speak, and when it was all said and done Plazo was arrested by the cops.

Courtney was hysterical. "Please don't take him away! It wasn't his fault!"

One of the officers said, "Are y'all gonna tell me what happened? Details?"

Silence.

"Well, since I'm not able to get what we need here, we'll sort shit out down at the police station."

Courtney felt dizzy.

Plazo had been her rock. And to have him taken away like this, would cripple her. Her desire for revenge brought danger to her doorstep.

It was settled.

She had to get out of the hospital. To find out what was going on with Plazo. But where was she going to go? And better yet, who would pick up Lawson?

Grabbing the phone, she made a call. She got the voicemail. "I don't know where you are brother, but I need you to go get your nephew. And keep an eye on him for me. They just took away Plazo. I gotta find out if they gonna let him go. Or if he needs bail." She sniffled. "Posea. I'm scared."

CHAPTER TWENTY-ONE

Courtney was still feeling the symptoms of her hospital stay and the stab wound.

Every step hurt. And so she had to be cautious due to the tenderness when she returned home with Lawson. The pain pills from the hospital were a small relief, but she didn't want to take too much because they clouded her mind and made her worry even more.

Her man, her rock, was still in prison days later, despite her telling the officials that he was not responsible. No one cared. At some point, it became obvious they just wanted to arrest Plazo versus finding out what really happened.

The best part about everything was that Ebony was arrested for stabbing her.

And since the police got involved with the incident at the hospital, she was sure she would not see Tye Gates either. Because the last thing he needed, was violating his parole.

As she opened the door to her home, something came over her. A sense of dread because she was greeted with the devastating condition of her house. Everything had been ransacked, stuff thrown everywhere, broken windows, fractured pictures.

They even pulled silverware out of the cabinets.

"Mom, what's going on?"

"We have to get out of here." Fear gripped her heart. As she quickly ushered Lawson back outside and into her car.

"Mom, who would do that?"

"Lawson, you're old enough to know that if I knew, I would tell you. Right now, I don't know what's happening."

Seeking refuge, Courtney checked into a luxury hotel with her son. She wanted to maintain some sense of normalcy for him. He may have been older, but she could tell by the look of him, that he was afraid and not just for himself, but for her too.

Once Lawson was settled, she stepped out of the hotel room to get him something to eat. She knew he didn't want anything big. He never had much of an appetite when things were bad. But she figured if he did eat anything junk would be it.

As she stood at the vending machine, waiting to make a selection, she saw Roberto, Jasmine's boyfriend.

"You Courtney, aren't you?"

She frowned. "Who are you?"

By T. STYLES

He stepped closer. And through clinched teeth, said, "Answer my question, bitch."

She stepped backwards. "No, I'm not."

He laughed. "Yeah, you Courtney." He slapped his chest, "I'm Roberto. You know who I am?"

She did remember the name. "What's this about?"

"Jasmine lost everything and couldn't make it back because of that streaming that you did live. That shit put a dent in my operations. I needed that business to make sure shit was right. And you owe me for that."

Courtney's heart raced. But she kept it together. "I don't owe you shit. Did your girlfriend tell you about all the shit she did to me before that moment?"

"So, you saying you're not gonna pay?"

"Pay for what?"

"Listen here." His voice was cold and menacing. "You're going to give me $50,000. When you do that, we gonna be good."

She shook her head. "Are you fucking crazy? I'm not paying you one single dime."

He laughed, an ominous look in his eye. "I think you should think it over. You don't want stuff worse. What we did to you today was only a small part of what we're going to do to you tomorrow."

"Stay away from me and stay away from my family!"

He shook his head and looked her dead in the eyes. "I want my money. I won't tell you again."

With that, he left. Once he was gone, Courtney rushed back to the room. She knew then she couldn't stay at the hotel.

"We got to go."

"Okay, mom, whatever you want."

The fact that Lawson was so easy at that moment gave her relief. In the past, she would have to tell him anything just to wear him down. Even coming over to the hotel, he asked a bunch of questions. But he must've saw in her eyes that something was serious, and that she needed him strong.

And strong he would be.

After all, he himself told her to fight.

When they made it to another hotel, she called her brother. "Posea, I need you and Yo-Yo to meet me at this hotel. It's about Roberto and the Glam Girls. Now this nigga's asking for money."

CHAPTER TWENTY-TWO

Mist descended over the streets of Washington DC as nightfall wrapped the city in an embrace. Streetlights cast a soft, diffused glow through the fog, creating halos of light that flickered in the damp air.

The atmosphere in Courtney's studio was heavy, and full of tension, as Courtney tried to come up with a plan. Adrienne, Yo-Yo, and Posea listened intently.

Adrienne was the first to speak. "I know you say you didn't want to pay him, but are you sure?"

Yo-Yo rolled her eyes. "Nah, that's not the move. She done said that already."

"What's most important is Lawson." Posea said. "Which is why I'm going to be at that school with him. I won't leave his side because I know they won't let me in the hallways. But when I tell you I'm going to be posted up in front of that building, know that I'm telling the truth. Won't nobody pull me from it."

Yo-Yo added her two cents. "And I've got some street contacts who can check out Roberto and Victor a little deeper. Since they know so much about us. It's time we got their deets too. And even Jasmine and Bree since we making a list."

Courtney felt overwhelmed with gratitude that her family was stepping up. But the conversation took another turn. "If you need someone to watch Lawson after school, I can take him with me back home." Yo-Yo offered.

"Damn, I wish you would leave this girl son alone."

Yo-Yo stared her down. "Say one more thing and I'm gonna drop you. Try me."

Silence.

"That's what the fuck I thought." She focused back on Courtney. "He'll be safe. The street's gonna see to that and won't no nigga crazy enough step on my block."

Courtney took a deep breath and hesitated. The thought of her son being in the projects in DC, even under Yo-Yo's extreme protection, made her sick.

"I appreciate it, Yo-Yo, but I can't. It's just too risky."

Yo-Yo shook her head. "When you gonna let him be with family? We out here. It ain't like you safe in the suburbs. They came through here and everything. But I guarantee you this," she looked down on the floor. "With your cousins on your father's side of the family watching him, he'll be good. Like right now why is he in the office sleep? He could be with his family."

She paused. "I mean, look at Posea. He been true blue from day one."

"Yo-Yo I hear you, but I just can't. And I know you know I love you."

Yo-Yo's face fell. Courtney hated putting it to her that way. And she hated seeing her cousin in pain, but she wasn't about to compromise when it came to Lawson's safety.

They all sat in silence for a minute, each lost in their own thoughts.

"Now let's get focused," Courtney continued.

The plan they were forming was dangerous because it gave no resolution. It was like Victor and Roberto still had the upper hand. Quietly, they all hoped it would work. And as the meeting dispersed, Courtney felt a heavy burden on her shoulders.

CHAPTER TWENTY-THREE

With the early arrival of winter, DC found itself blanketed in a thin layer of snow on the cold November night.

Under the neon glow of a red and silver sign, Courtney's favorite diner buzzed with life in the heart of the evening. The sizzle of burgers on the grill mixed with the clatter of plates and the lively chatter of patrons, while the sweet aroma of freshly brewed coffee and warm apple pie filled the air.

Yo-Yo and Courtney sat down for dinner at a cozy spot with Lawson happily seated at the nearby table enjoying his meal surrounded by Yo-Yo's baby fathers standing and watching. In front of him was Yo-Yo's eldest son, and Courtney wondered if it was a sneaky way to make an introduction without her approval.

For now she let it slide.

The atmosphere was casual but Courtney sensed Yo-Yo had something more on her heart than just a friendly meal.

"Listen, I need to talk to you about something." Yo-Yo began, her tone serious. "I've had the streets keeping tabs on Bree and Jazz. They haven't been home in a month, and I hear they cut ties with Victor and Roberto so them niggas may be moving solo."

Courtney leaned closer, "So what you think happened? Like, if they were broken up, why would Roberto be at the hotel? You don't think they did something to them, do you?"

"That's not my problem. But you are."

Courtney respected that answer. Their conversation was interrupted by the waitress, prompting Courtney to ask for some privacy.

"Listen, can you give us 20 minutes? If you want you can just take care of our sons right there. We just really need a little privacy on this end."

When she walked away and smiled, Yo-Yo dropped the biggest bombshell.

"But that's not why I want to talk to you. I think Adrienne is a snake, and you shouldn't trust her."

Where was this coming from? She didn't even tell her she was looking in on her friend. "A snake?" Courtney was disgusted. "You mean my Adrienne Burton?"

"If that's what you want to call her."

"First of all, why you looking into her?"

"Because, like I said, I don't trust her."

"But I didn't tell you to do that."

"At this point, everybody's a suspect."

"So you go against me. And check on somebody who been in my corner from day one. I've known her longer than I known you, Yo-Yo."

"Can you listen to me?"

"Fuck that! I need everybody in my corner, in my corner. So why are you trying to take somebody out?"

"You think I'm just a dumb thug bitch, don't you? That I would do something just to weaken the people that's around you."

"If that's what you want to call it, let it be that!"

"You know, ever since you asked for my help," Yo-Yo said. "I've been here. I never once turned my back on you. And just because I do a little investigation to make sure your friend is not the ops, you get mad with me?"

"I'm mad because you supposed to have been looking at Victor and Roberto, not Adrienne. And if you don't see it that way—"

"You know what...I'm done." Yo-Yo stood up.

"This is not what I want, but if it needs to be that way, know that this is all on you," Courtney yelled.

"Don't call me, don't reach out. And since you want to act like your father's side of the family don't exist, consider me dead to you." She grabbed her purse and looked at her son. "Come on, Sean." Before she walked out, she looked at Lawson. "I'm sorry we didn't get a chance to know each other, cousin. And more than anything I'm sorry you had to hear us like this. But when you get older and want to meet your grandfather's side of the family, we will be waiting." She looked at Courtney once more and stormed out.

When she left, Courtney noticed the small piece of yellow folded paper on the table. Yo-Yo's hand had been covering it, so she didn't see it before. Pulling the paper closer to her, she was afraid to open it.

Lawson sat across from her. "You good, Ma?"

She didn't answer.

She just turned over the paper and saw a name that made her sick.

Not Adrienne Burton. Adrienne Davenport.

Having known the name, she threw up right where she sat.

CHAPTER TWENTY-FOUR

The wind whipped mercilessly through the streets. People moved briskly, scarves fluttering, while the chill sucked out their souls.

Confused about what Yo-Yo had written, Courtney met Posea at the diner. Although shit was normally smooth, the tension between them was palpable. Posea's expression was serious, his usual easy-going demeanor replaced by a sternness that Courtney rarely saw in her brother.

"We need to talk about how the fuck you treated Yo-Yo," Posea started. "You were wrong. She's been nothing but loyal, and you know it."

Courtney shifted uncomfortably, guilt and defensiveness weighing heavy. "I know, but you know how I am with trust. It's not easy for me, Pose. And I didn't ask her to do what she did. Now I realize I have somebody around me. Who's a snake but—."

"So let me get this straight, you're mad about her identifying a snake in your camp? And because she told you."

"It's just—."

"We family. Yo-Yo, me, we've been in this with you from the start. And she deserved better."

The fear that Posea might turn his back on her crept into Courtney's mind. She couldn't afford to lose him, not now. "You're not...you're not gonna bail on me, are you?"

He looked at her, his eyes softening. "I'm not going anywhere, sis. But you need to make shit right with Yo-Yo." He pointed at her. "If not, there's only so much I can do. Because if I knew you were going to hurt Yo-Yo, I would've never linked y'all up. They're very few real bitches in the world. We're lucky to have her."

The conversation lingered heavily in the air. Posea reached into his jacket and pulled out a piece of paper, handing it to Courtney. "This is Tye Gates' address."

Courtney took the paper. "That was quick."

Posea met her gaze squarely. "It's time you face shit head-on, Court. So I'm glad you wanted his address. Because this thing with Tye, it's all part of this mess."

"You think I should go and see him? Like is it safe?"

"I can't help you with that anymore. Only you spent time with that man in the past. Only you know if he has malice in his heart. I don't care how many years passed."

Courtney stared at the address, her mind racing. "Thank you."

"I love you, girl."

She stood up, kissed his cheek, and walked out.

Tye Gates stood under the hot spray of the shower, his thoughts swirling as the comfort of the warm water reminded him he was home. The tattoos on his light brown skin were many, including the italicized tattoo that ripped across his forehead which read DOMINION. He had plans to cover that up. The second ran along his left cheek read POWER and the third on the right side read RULE.

The artwork, so blatant, connected to one another with brown vines. To be clear it was beautiful to observe and at the same time off- putting and scary.

Freedom felt unfamiliar and now he was grappling with the reality of his new life. His job delivering pizzas and fast food was a far cry from his previous lavish lifestyle selling dope or owning a club, but it was

By T. STYLES

honest work, and he appreciated the normalcy it brought.

As he stepped out of the shower, wrapping a towel around his waist, a knock at his door caught him off guard. He wasn't expecting visitors. Quickly he got himself together and rushed to the front door. Peering through the peephole, his surprise deepened...it was Courtney.

Opening the door, he managed to mask his shock. "Courtney? How did you—"

She cut him off, her tone urgent. "We need to talk, Tye. Now."

"Sure, let me get dressed." He ushered her inside.

His place was cute. A one-bedroom apartment just big enough for a man who was trying to find his way. Brown furniture. Accessories. A TV. A couch...the basics.

As Courtney took her seat, she wasted no time, diving straight into the heart of the matter. "What you want from me, Tye?"

Tye held her gaze, his expression earnest. "Nothing material, Courtney. I just...I want to be a part of Lawson's life. That's all."

Courtney studied him for a moment, searching for any hint of deceit. "Are you sure?"

"I promise." He placed two hands on his heart. "I'm not trying to cause you trouble."

"How did you know his name?"

"He goes to school with a friend of mine's son. They're cool. That's how I knew it. But I never overstepped boundaries or tried to get him to connect us in anyway. I wouldn't do that."

Finding that he was being real, she nodded slowly. "For some reason, I believe you. But there's something else. Another reason why I'm here."

"I'm listening."

"Adrienne Davenport, she's been close to me, too close. It's like I've had her around me all these years. Help me build my business. And she's..."

Tye's face was drained of color. "Davenport? You mean Joanne's sister?"

Courtney nodded. "I didn't know which Davenport she was. Until just now."

"What the fuck is wrong with her?" He stood up and walked toward the kitchen. "She was kind of quiet. Not like Joanne or her other sisters. But I don't know what she wants with you. I will say it's strange as fuck." He scratched his head. "Get rid of her."

"Not yet. I need to see what she's about first."

"You better than me because that bitch would be history. You want anything to drink?"

"None for me."

He returned with a soda over ice. And she was shocked. Because if he liked anything, it was his liquor.

"Is there anything else I should know?"

He breathe deeply. "The Davenports are dangerous. Not just dangerous in a loose sense. They treacherous. So what has she been doing around you?"

"She's an engineer for my podcast. She never even brings you up unless I do. So it would be impossible for me to know that she knew you."

His eyebrows rose. "You still talk about me?"

"Not like that. But I have talked about you on my podcast. And all the things you did to me."

"Really am sorry about that. And I want you to know that I'm serious." He looked down hating that the whole basis for her success was his failure as a man. He turned the subject over. "I mean I was supposed to marry Joanne. When you and I got into our situation, with that diary, she lost everything. And if her sister is in the mix, it sounds like she blames you for it."

"I've been having people do some weird shit to me over the past year. Now I know who it is. It wasn't the Glam Girls. It wasn't Mommy Moves. Or even the Liberation League."

"The Liberation League? Them brothers not into all this shit."

"At one point I didn't know. But I believe it now."

Tye leaned back, concern all over his face. "Whatever you need from me, you got it."

Courtney took a deep breath, her mind working through the implications. "I got myself into this, I have to get myself out of it."

"What about my son? I'm serious about building a bond with him."

"I'm working on a plan, Tye. For Lawson. But it needs to be on my terms. Can you respect that?"

He nodded, a newfound understanding in his eyes. "I'll wait on your call. I just respect you even coming over here. As far as the Davenport's, shit won't go as you think. They got money. A lot of it. And they can do things to you that you can only dream of. Be careful."

CHAPTER TWENTY-FIVE

Dear Diary,

My life is crashing down around me.

Sakura and Yo-Yo were right.

Adrienne came to me in the early days, right after Tye was arrested. I remember wanting to start a podcast to help people out of the predicaments that they were in. I wanted them to know that someone was there to fight for them, like nobody ever did me.

I should have saw her coming.

She was pretty, smart, and too eager. She even came with some money to help me get new mics, new chairs, and new equipment. I was so green back then. So in need of companionship, and it was a woman, so course I felt safe.

Wrong.

She been playing me in the background. I'm questioning everything.

Did anybody really pull up in front of the studio?

Was she the one leaving shit on my doorstep? Scratching my car? Stuff like that?

And now my boyfriend is locked up.

My new friend is in jail.

And I'm not talking to Yo-Yo, someone who had been riding for me from day one.

What am I going to do? How can I get out of this situation?

To top it all off, I've been keeping Lawson at hotels while I run errands. And then threatening him within every inch of his life to prevent him from leaving out.

He don't deserve that shit and I know it. But fear has me acting this way.

This anxiety of leaving him alone causes me to rush and not always think straight. Several times I almost got into an accident because I don't want to leave him too long.

But I guess it is what it is for now.

I'm looking for a break.

By T. STYLES

CHAPTER TWENTY-SIX

The afternoon sun cast a soft, golden light over the DC projects, tempering the fall chill with its faint warmth. The sound of people talking echoed in the courtyards, mingling with distant music from open windows.

Suddenly, one of Yo-Yo's phones rang. With the number she knew, but in context was still weird to receive. "Everything good," Yo-Yo asked as she sat on the edge of her bed. "Since when have you called to take my order?"

"I'm calling about something else."

Yo-Yo rose up. "You have my attention."

"Them dudes that came by my restaurant to get you, maybe about to snatch your little cousin."

"How you sound?"

"Sounds like they put a bounty on the boys head. It's going down today. There was a lot of talk last night when people didn't think I was listening. At first I didn't know who they were talking about but this morning someone said something to Stacker. And it sounds legit. What have you gotten yourself mixed in?"

"Too much to list."

"Well, you need to get a hold of your people. ASAP!"

The mere thought of Lawson being targeted by Roberto and Victor sent a jolt of fear through her. Why wouldn't these niggas leave them alone? She hung up without even thinking.

Dialing Courtney repeatedly, she was frustrated that each call went to voicemail, deepening her anxiety. "Fuck! Where are you?"

Cursing under her breath, Yo-Yo paced back and forth. She felt isolated and helpless, knowing that all her baby fathers, the men she could usually rely on for muscle, were tied up in business on the other side of town. They were at least an hour away, too far to be of immediate help.

The frustration was mounting, almost choking her. She needed to think, to plan. Grabbing a drink from the nearby counter, she took a long steadying gulp. Should she call the school and let them know? Or would they think she was crazy since she didn't have any concrete proof? She couldn't just grab her little cousin up out of school because Courtney made it clear. She wanted her to stay the fuck away from her son.

She looked at her phone again, willing it to ring, to be Courtney on the other end confirming that Lawson was safe.

But the call never came.

In the dimly lit hotel room, Courtney lay sprawled on the bed, a deep sleep enveloping her. The pain medicine for her stab wound, taken in an attempt to dull not just the physical pain but the emotional turmoil as well, had knocked her out.

Over the past few days the hotel had become her temporary refuge, a place where she could find some semblance of peace, away from the unsteady and dangerous reality at home. And lately, the only true respite she found was in brief moments of sleep, especially when she knew Lawson was safe in school.

Exhausted, her phone, which she had plugged into the charger before crashing, lay disconnected from the wall socket. The battery had drained to empty, cutting her off from any calls or messages. In her vulnerable state, she was oblivious to the potential dangers that loomed outside her hotel room, and unaware of Yo-Yo's frantic attempts to reach her.

The room was quiet, save for the soft hum of the radiator and Courtney's steady breathing. The curtains were drawn, keeping the chaos of the outside world at bay.

The sleep was too good.

So good that she eventually felt it.

Courtney's heart raced as she bolted up from the bed. Glancing at the clock, panic set in, she had just fifteen minutes to get to Lawson's school and in her haste, she grabbed her phone, and realized it hadn't charged while she slept. With no time to waste, she snatched her keys and dashed out the room.

The hotel's elevator seemed to mock her urgency, so without hesitation, she opted for the stairs, taking them two at a time in her frantic descent. Bursting out of the hotel, she sprinted to her Benz which had just been repaired and sped off toward the school.

It took forever, but eventually she arrived, her eyes frantically scanned the dispersing crowd for her boy. Her heart sank as she realized as the crowd was reduced to no more than ten that he was nowhere in sight. Quickly, she entered the school and questioned everybody who passed her way. Janitors included.

They all told her the same thing that Lawson left earlier.

Rushing back to her car, she plugged her phone into the car charger, willing it to come to life faster. It was at 15%.

Just enough to make a few calls.

First, she dialed Posea, her fingers trembling. He would've been at the school, but he had a wisdom tooth issue that was wreaking havoc on his world. He was going to get it extracted earlier that day. Which meant now, he was probably out cold.

She also thought about her cousin. Though Yo-Yo had not spoken to her since they separated at the diner, she dialed Yo-Yo's number anyway, but to her dismay it went straight to voicemail.

What the fuck was going on?

She started to call the police, but it felt like an inside thing. She didn't wanna go there just yet unless she was sure.

Driven by instincts, Courtney made the decision to speed over to the projects. She didn't know why, but her heart was telling her to go in that direction. As she navigated through the city streets, every scenario played out in her mind, each more terrifying than the last.

Yo-Yo was being chased. After grabbing her little cousin Lawson from school, to avoid his kidnapping, she separated from the pack and was alone. She didn't have anybody to watch her back but she would protect him with her whole life.

"I'm sorry I gotta drive this fast, but somebody—"

"I see what's going on!" He looked behind him and back at her. "Do what you gotta do, cuz!"

She nodded, proud that he was being strong.

"I'm going to this restaurant called the Jerk off. Hopefully I can get some help there." Then she looked at him. "But if something happens to me, I need you to go by yourself."

"Go where?"

"To the restaurant. But don't go into the front. Go around the back and tell them you're Yo-Yo's cousin. They're gonna get you where you need to be."

The car behind them was getting closer. So close she felt they were about to crash into her. When she squinted through the rearview mirror, she saw Roberto and Victor's faces.

Her blood ran cold. Because they were literally the worst things that she and her crew ever did.

"Who they?"

"I don't want you to worry about that. But nothing is going to happen to you."

"Is something going to happen to you?"

"Something happen to Yo-Yo? Picture that! I'm made of—"

Suddenly a bullet came flying from the back window, sending the car careening into another car. Blood splattered everywhere, even on Lawson's face. With wide eyes, when he looked behind him through the destroyed glass, he saw two cars. At least four men with guns hanging from their hands approached from the back.

Remembering what his cousin said about the restaurant, he exited and ran.

And when I say he ran, he ran fast. The football practice that he'd been doing to become a wide receiver definitely took hold. He was gone so quickly they couldn't catch him in their dreams.

But he was still a child. And he was so afraid he could barely breathe. Like somebody was beating on his lungs with five fists.

But it didn't matter.

He would do what his cousin told him.

He would survive.

No matter what.

As Courtney pulled up at the projects, the scene was chaotic – a sea of faces, many unfamiliar. Just distant relatives from her father's side and residents. As she took it all in, she noticed the air was heavy with tension. She couldn't pinpoint the source of the turmoil, but she knew something was terribly wrong.

After she parked, before she could process her surroundings, a man she didn't recognize grabbed her, guiding her forcefully towards a car. Shock and confusion rendered her speechless and questions swirled in her mind.

None found their way to her lips. How could you verbalize fear properly without passing out?

She was teetering on the edge of a nervous breakdown, her world spinning uncontrollably. So she didn't fight. For the moment something felt eerily safe.

The car journey was a blur as they arrived at a nondescript building, and she was ushered inside.

Relief.

Somewhat.

Because there, she saw some of Yo-Yo's baby fathers and her brother, Posea. Wanting help, Courtney rushed into Posea's arms, her voice trembling. "What's going on? I can't find Lawson!"

Posea's eyes were filled with a sadness that confirmed her worst fears even before he spoke. He gripped her lovingly by the arms. "Something happened." He led her inside the apartment. "Let's do this first."

One of Yo-Yo's baby fathers emerged from a room with Lawson at his side. The sight of her son, his clothes stained with blood, sent Courtney crashing to her knees.

Lawson ran into her arms, his body trembling. He used his young man, strength to keep his mother steady. He smelt of metal and sweat, and she didn't care. Courtney held him tightly and amidst her relief that Lawson was safe, the devastating news hit her – Yo-Yo was gone.

She separated from him. "Are you Okay."

"I am but—"

Posea knelt beside her, his voice choked with emotion. "Yo-Yo... she didn't make it, Courtney. She stood her ground for Lawson. She saved him, but..."

The reality that Yo-Yo had sacrificed her life for Lawson was overwhelming. Guilt, grief, and gratitude engulfed Courtney. Yo-Yo had defied her orders, fought for her son, and paid the ultimate price. After hearing how it went down, she had an out of body experience.

In a whisper, she said, "This all my fault."

"Listen, bitch, I love you, but what you not gonna do is this right here," Posea said. "Not when the niggas who loved her more than anything, lost a real one. Not when her sons have to move in life without a mother. Honor her life by taking care of Lawson. And more than anything by being strong."

He was right.

Now was not the right time.

As Courtney clutched her son, the world shattered. Yo-Yo's bravery and final act of protection would be etched in her heart forever. Courtney knew one thing for certain, Yo-Yo's sacrifice would not be in vain.

CHAPTER TWENTY-SEVEN

Dear Diary,

I can't believe how much has gone down.

I can't believe the sacrifice Yo-Yo made. After me telling her not to be around my son, she did it anyway and saved his life.

And because of it, my days seem bland, colorless. We can't even stay at our house, hopping from place to place, trying to "be safe".

The other day I saw this dude on the way to get Lawson some fried chicken. I jumped when I first heard him call my name. But relaxed a little when I knew who it was.

He was somebody I was dating after I was released from prison. But when he saw me recently, he said I looked bad. Like, that was the first thing he said when he walked up.

And when I initially got released from prison, I looked bad, so what he was saying was, I must've looked worse.

That was the condition of my life.

The girl Adrienne called me every day, but I don't answer. She says she heard about what happened to my cousin and that she wishes me the best.

But I don't trust her, however, I'm not willing to release her into the wild either. So I don't tell her anything.

I'm still unsure how to handle her.

I guess I'll see, but it's going to be based on what she wants from me. And what I can get from her.

By T. STYLES

CHAPTER TWENTY-EIGHT

I n the gritty city nights, within a motel, Courtney found herself unraveling. With everything going on she still hadn't heard Plazo's voice. And now, meals went uneaten, and sleep was a stranger. The only rest she got was in a stiff chair in the motel room, watching over Lawson like a hawk. Vowing to never let him out of her sight which drove him insane.

At least he didn't have any problems sleeping.

She couldn't say the same for herself.

Outside, the constant hum of the city was interrupted by the occasional siren or the distant chatter of night owls. Posea, ever the loyal brother, stood guard in his car, to ensure their safety. Even though she told him he didn't need to. The reason they were in the motel instead of the hotel was because Posea wanted to keep eyes on the room. And in a Luxury hotel, he was concerned that things would miss his view.

But, one night, unable to bear the sight of Posea's unwavering loyalty, she opened the door. The car was parked directly in front of the window. "Posea, come on. You can't keep doing this."

He rolled the window down. "I'm good little sis."

"If you're going to be here you're going to be inside. So, please come in. I'm not gonna be able to get rest with you in that car. You can watch us from in here anyway."

He resisted at first but eventually relented, making a makeshift bed on the floor next to the door. His presence in the room was both a comfort and a reminder of the dangers lurking.

The next morning, she decided she needed some air.

"Where you going?" Posea asked from the floor.

"I'll be safe. I just need to get out for one second. Keep eyes on your nephew."

"Okay but leave your phone on. I'm not fucking around."

Leaving Posea and Lawson in the safety of the room, Courtney slipped out. She didn't have a plan. She just drove aimlessly, the city's neon lights blurring past her until she found herself at her aunt's grave. It was still dark out. Almost pitch black. The cemetery was a sea of silence, broken only by the rustling of leaves in the early morning breeze.

Standing there, lost in thought, she couldn't shake the feeling of being at a crossroads. Her aunt had always been her moral compass, her guide through life's toughest moments. Now, more than anything, she needed guidance.

Tears flowed.

Harder than ever.

It turned out to be unbearable.

And so she decided to go to her house. To see if it was still standing. On the outside it was there but what did the inside look like? Did strangers take over like they seemed to do her life?

When she opened the door, she was slightly angry with herself. Because, despite the strangers ruining her home, she could've cleaned up. She could've put things back in order.

But she left the broken glass, fractured wood, and things that were once safe in drawers, scattered everywhere.

Just like her life.

As she stood there, a spark of something - an idea, a plan, maybe even a way out began to form in her mind. It was like a puzzle piece clicking into place, a missing part of a larger scheme she hadn't seen before.

She also realized there were no guarantees that she would come out on the right side of things. Besides, most of what happened was her fault. She allowed herself to get caught up in a game without being clear on who was the villain.

As a result, it meant she was.

Back at the motel, as she looked at Posea and Lawson, a protective fierceness took hold.

Courtney Martin, once a victim of circumstance, was about to become a villain with purpose. She would only hit those who attacked and she had no intentions on missing. The night was still young, and the city, with all its shadows and secrets, was the perfect backdrop for her plan to unfold.

By T. STYLES

CHAPTER TWENTY-NINE

Courtney revved up her car. Lawson was safe with her brother, and now it was time for her to handle some other business. Her destination was the county prison, to visit her friend Sakura who was doing time.

The drive over allowed her moments of reflection and she felt a sense of strength coursing through her veins. She was on a mission, and nothing was going to stand in her way.

Pulling into the parking lot, she left her purse in the trunk, but grabbed a small see-through pink change purse filled with ones and fives. The only things she was allowed to take inside for her visit. Before entering, she glanced at the imposing structure of the jail, steeling herself for what was ahead.

Visiting an inmate was the most demeaning process you could imagine. It's like the system punished you for still caring about someone behind bars. Like they wanted you to forget them, or even blame you for them being in prison in the first place.

Once inside, she signed in at the front desk visitor log, the guard instructed her to remove her shoes and empty her pockets. If they suspected you had anything on you illegal you could find yourself in the side room removing all your clothing.

Which could also mean being locked up. Every step felt invasive, but she kept her composure, her focus on seeing Sakura.

When she took her seat, a stank hit her—disinfectant and despair. The odor seemed to cling to the walls and the people within causing her belly to spin.

"Martin, Courtney!" A guard called out.

"I'm right here!

"Let's go!"

She rose and walked through to the visiting area, her heart heavy. Other visitors followed her too close for comfort. Most were young women and younger men who she was certain were a lot of the inmates sons.

When she finally made it to the hall, there, sitting across from her, was Sakura. She was dressed in the usual orange jumpsuit, her hands clasped in front of her.

What Courtney saw next enraged her beyond belief.

The sight of her friend, beaten up, a black eye, a bruised lip, struck hard. The marks appeared old but spoke volumes of the harshness she was enduring in prison.

Denise was involved. She felt it in her heart.

Courtney opened her mouth but closed it right away. Slowly she walked toward her. "So I speak to you almost every day and you didn't tell me this?"

"Didn't want you to worry. Don't want you to worry now."

"So what happened? Who did this?"

Silence.

"Sakura, what happened to you?"

"I have some more months here. I gotta do my time how I gotta do my time. So in this visiting room can we at least pretend like nothing back there exists?"

"But I can help you."

"Courtney, don't you see? It's time to help yourself."

That hit heavy. But was also laced with truth. "Let me first tell you, that you were right. Adrienne is a snake."

"Not surprised. What are you gonna do about it?"

Courtney took a deep breath. "I've got a plan. And you're a part of it because I want to put this behind us once and for all."

Sakura's bruised face lit up. Grateful for Courtney's loyalty. "Court, you know I'm with you too. Whatever you need."

Sakura's eyes kept roaming to the change purse in her hands. "Good. But first, let me get you something from the vending machine. What you craving?"

Sakura chuckled, a glimmer of her old self shining through. "Some of those chips. A soda. Anything else you see good over there because this prison food ain't cutting it."

As Courtney told her the plan, while Sakura ate chips, a smile spread across her face. It seemed as if Courtney had thought of everything. Seeing each detail to the finish line.

The visit might have been in a grim setting, but for Courtney, it reinforced the bond she had with Sakura – a bond that no jail walls could break. She was building an alliance, and Sakura was a key piece.

The plan was taking shape, and Courtney was ready to see it through.

And that was on Yo-Yo.

CHAPTER THIRTY

Courtney stepped into Posea's apartment for the first time, taking in the contemporary style of his living space. The color scheme was a sleek blend of black and gold, giving off a vibe that was both modern and comfortable. Despite their close bond over the years, this was her first glimpse into his personal world, and it surprised her how meticulously neat everything was.

"Damn, brother! I didn't know you had a little taste for decoration."

"It wasn't me. It was him."

Suddenly, she hated that she brought it up. The breakup was still heavy she could tell.

"Come inside. Are you hungry?"

"Actually, I am."

"Where's Lawson?"

"I left him in the room by himself. He's 15-years-old and I guess I'm gonna have to trust it sooner or later."

He smiled. "Whoa! That was huge and I know it wasn't easy but I'm happy to see you coming around. Because my little nigga solid. He ain't gonna cause no problems for you. Not right now anyway."

Posea, clad in jeans that hung low enough to reveal the band of his boxers, moved around the kitchen shirtless, revealing an array of tattoos that decorated his torso. Courtney watched as he expertly put together a sandwich, the ease of his movements showing a side of him she rarely saw.

When he handed her the sandwich, Courtney took a bite and was instantly impressed. "This might be the best sandwich I've ever had," she said, genuine surprise in her voice.

"Go ahead with that shit."

"I'm serious. I should've come over here before."

"I didn't give you the invitation before."

She thought about it and he was right. "Yeah, why haven't you given me an invite?"

He wiped a counter. "Because this always been my place of peace. Every person should have one. Technically it could be your house. But sometimes it's the person you care about." He looked away and she could tell he went somewhere deep.

As she ate, her eyes caught sight of something that moved her profoundly. There, inked on Posea's chest, were two names – hers and Lawson's. She touched the names gently, her voice soft. "You have our names tattooed on your body?"

Posea looked down at his chest and then back at her, a small smile playing on his lips. He had forgotten all about it. "Yeah, you're family, Courtney. I put the people who mean the most to me close to my heart."

The sentiment struck a chord, her eyes brimming tears. She quickly composed herself. "I appreciate everything you've done for us, Posea. For me."

Silence.

She then shifted the conversation to the matter at hand. "Now I need you to make a connection. With the rest of the family."

Posea's expression turned serious. "You mean our family?"

"Yes, our family. If I'm going to do this, I need y'all."

He scratched his head. "It's gonna be tough, but I'll do what I have to. We in this together."

CHAPTER THIRTY-ONE

The drive to Yo-Yo's place was silent, with Courtney and Posea each lost in their own thoughts. Every now and again, he would look over at her and squeeze her hand. And when he did that, she would let out a deep sigh. It was almost as if he knew that she wasn't breathing fully.

When they arrived at the apartment building, the atmosphere was thick. It seems like every one outside had their eyes on Courtney. Their looks seem to be filled with disappointment.

Making it up the stairs, she saw people coming out of their apartments. Posea nodded at a few of them and shook a few more hands. But no one said anything to her.

It was like she was the streets pariah.

When they made it to Yo-Yo's front door, she paused.

Posea told her, "You gotta stay strong."

She smiled and he opened the door.

The house was filled with Yo-Yo's three baby fathers and her three sons, all gathered in the living room, showcasing the impact Yo-Yo had on their lives.

They were waiting on her. Wanting to hear what she had to say.

Courtney stepped into the center and her brother hung back, leaving her to take the journey alone. Feeling the weight of her words before she even spoke, she looked at each of the men.

"First, I need to say I'm sorry," Courtney began, her voice steady, filled with genuine remorse. "Truly sorry."

"What you apologizing for?" Baby father #3 said glaring her way.

"For everything that's happened, for any part I played in bringing danger to our doorstep."

The first two baby fathers nodded, their faces showing understanding and a silent acceptance of her apology. The third, however, was more reserved, his eyes hard but not unkind.

"I hear what you saying, Courtney," he said. "But once this is over, I don't want anything else to do with you."

"I really—"

"I don't need to hear anything else. What fucks me up is that you acted like you were too good for this part of your family. And she died because of that shit!"

Posea got in the mix. "You gotta hear her out, Nic—."

Courtney turned around and silenced her brother. This was her fight and she would stay on it.

He nodded and stood back against the wall.

Courtney met Baby father #3's gaze, recognizing and respecting his pain. "I understand," she replied sincerely. "I made judgments. Based off my own fear and insecurities. But nobody ever cared about me that strongly upon just meeting except Yo-Yo. I mean, how did she do that? Love so fully."

"I don't have the answer to that. But it will be something I strive to possess for the rest of my life. She loved me despite myself. That's what you call unconditional."

They all nodded.

She wiped the tears forming in her eyes. "But just so you know, I'm gonna always be here. I don't care what her sons need. Money, support, my blood, my kidney, I'm going to be here! My actions will show you where my heart lies. Swear on my life!"

Baby father, #3 nodded. In that moment she could see she reached a place in his heart only real bitches knew.

"Now I want to make them pay! You don't take somebody out like her and move on with life!"

"Ain't nobody been fucking with us yet." Baby father #1 said.

"That's the thing with these dudes. They hang back and wait. So they may not be fucking with you now, but they could fuck with you in the near future. If we don't stop them."

Taking a deep breath, Courtney laid out her plan. She spoke with clarity and conviction, outlining each step and the role everyone would play. Her plan was bold, risky, and required a level of trust and cooperation from everyone present.

And as she detailed her strategy, the room listened intently. There was a sense of unity, a common goal that bound them together in the wake of Yo-Yo's sacrifice.

When she finished, the room was silent for a moment before Posea stood up, affirming his support. One by one, Yo-Yo's baby fathers agreed to play their part, even the one who had expressed his desire to distance himself after everything was said and done.

The meeting concluded on some real shit.

And as she looked around the room at the faces of those who had become her unlikely allies, she felt a surge of hope.

Even if bullets had to fly.

The night had enveloped the city, casting long shadows on the streets as Courtney drove, with Lawson quietly seated beside her. They moved through the landscapes of DC, driving from the well-lit, luxurious areas into the grittier, rawer parts of the town. The transition was hard hitting – million-dollar buildings gave way to weathered structures, and the clean lines of big money faded into the rugged edges of just enough to survive.

Lawson, usually full of questions and observations, sat silently beside his mother. He sensed the gravity of the moment, understanding in his young way that she needed his silent support more than his curiosity and loaded questions.

As they entered the projects, a familiar ruggedness came into view. Lawson's demeanor changed as they pulled up and saw Yo-Yo's three baby fathers and his cousin Sean, whom he had met at the diner.

A smile broke on his face. "Ma, for real?"

"I'm not going to lie, Lawson. I'm scared about your independence. It's not because I don't believe you're strong enough. I do. But if something were to happen to you, I don't—"

"I know what this meant for you. And I'm not going to let you down. I'm going to show you how you raised me."

He hugged Courtney tightly, a wordless expression of love and assurance.

Getting out the car, Lawson was warmly welcomed by the baby fathers, each introducing him to their sons...his cousins. The first baby father, Sean's pops, dapped him up, the second introduced him to Rico, and the third to Nathaniel. It was a gathering of family, bound not just by blood but by shared understanding that shit was about to pop off.

Sean's father gestured for Lawson to follow them upstairs. He was on his way but rushed back to give her a fierce hug before disappearing into the building with his newfound cousins.

Baby father #2 turned to Courtney, his voice reassuring. "He'll be safe here, Courtney. Nothing gets through that building, not even a swat team unless we say so. And we don't say so."

Courtney glanced around and noticed a group of formidable-looking men positioned strategically around the building. It was clear they were ready for anything, their presence a silent vow to protect and honor Yo-Yo's memory.

"Thank you," Courtney said, her voice thick with gratitude.

As she prepared to leave, Baby father #3 approached. He placed a hand on her shoulder, a gesture that spoke volumes. Without a word, he walked away.

With her son, safe, she got into her car. Knowing that he was surrounded by family, she was ready to put her plan into action. At one point she hid herself. But now, she was willing to put her life on the line.

Tye was gearing up for his new day, a routine that had become his anchor since his release, when an

By T. STYLES

unexpected knock at his door jolted him. Opening it, he found Courtney standing on the other side.

For a brief moment, a smile flickered on his face, a fleeting reminder of a time before their world had turned upside down.

And then he remembered they were possibly enemies.

Or were they?

He stepped aside. Courtney's demeanor was intense. "I'm about to set off a plan, Tye. A plan that...might cost me everything," she confessed, her voice steady but filled with fears.

Tye watched her, the weight of her words sinking in. "What you need from me?"

She looked him straight in the eyes. "I need to know what kind of father you plan to be to Lawson."

Silence.

"Tye!"

"Come with me."

Instead of answering directly, Tye turned to his computer and pulled up a banking website. There, he showed her two trust funds – one for $25,000 and another for $50,000, set up for Lawson. His name plain for her to see.

"This is for him. I've been saving up, not just from what I earned inside, but also from old street debts that were finally paid. People owed me, and I put it to good use. That's one of the reasons why I'm in this apartment. I could be somewhere different. But I want what's good for my son's future. Like my father never did for me."

Courtney's eyes widened in surprise as Tye continued, opening another tab on his computer to reveal an application for vocational school. "I'm enrolling to learn about air-conditioning and heating systems. I'm trying to build a life, a legitimate one. For my kid."

It was what she wanted to hear.

Overwhelmed, Courtney broke down, tears streaming down her face. She didn't know what she expected, but she definitely didn't think Tye, who was once the most selfish man in the world, was thinking about a relationship with her child.

He hadn't even met him yet.

Tye hesitated for a moment before reaching out and holding her, a gesture that bridged the gap of years of beef. The moment was long, and she hated herself for giving in so quickly.

But it felt like forgiveness.

The most powerful elixir in the world.

Courtney, gathering herself together, looked up at Tye. "Promise me, if I don't make it out of this, that you'll step up. That you'll keep Lawson connected to my father's side of the family. Even if it means dealing with Posea."

Tye sighed, the very mention of Posea bringing a shadow of resentment. The man did some pretty vicious things to Tye. Including taking out one of his best friends. So the part of having a killer around his son was not going over easy.

"Dealing with your brother...that's gonna take a new level of maturity I'm not sure I have right now. But for everyone else, I'll make sure Lawson knows them. As for Posea, I gotta pray on that shit."

"I guess I gotta accept that. But he's good to him, Tye. I just want you to know that." She hesitated, then added, "There's one more thing I need."

Tye looked at her, ready to listen. "Just say the word."

Courtney stood in the middle of her house, the destruction around her a reminder of the chaos that had infiltrated her life. The moon cast a pale light through broken windows as she began the task of cleaning, determined to reclaim her home.

In the living room, debris was scattered everywhere – shattered glass from a broken coffee table, overturned chairs, cushions ripped open with their stuffing spilling out like open wounds. Pictures that once hung proudly on the wall now lay on the floor, their frames cracked, happy memories destroyed but not forgotten.

Moving to the kitchen, Courtney found silverware strewn across the floor, mixed with broken dishes and scattered food items. Methodically, she began picking up each piece, cleaning and organizing them back into drawers. The simple act of restoring order gave her a small sense of control.

The bathroom was less damaged but still showed signs of intrusion. Towels were flung about, toiletry items knocked over and spilled. Courtney worked quietly, tidying up, rearranging everything back to its rightful place.

Lawson's room was next.

Video games and books were out of sort, but nothing was irreparably damaged. She carefully put each item back on the shelves, straightened his bed, and rehung posters that had fallen down. The room soon looked like it did before...a young man's haven.

Finally, she moved to her own bedroom. The mattress had been flipped, drawers emptied, clothes thrown around. She set out about putting everything back, folding clothes, and arranging her personal items.

With the house now in relative order, the lingering sense of violation still hung heavy in the air. Seeking solace, Courtney decided to take a bath. The warm water and the solitude of the bathroom offered a brief escape. Her fully charged phone sat nearby, a connection to the outside world.

To her son if he called.

As she soaked, lost in thought, her phone did ring. She almost dropped the handset in the water.

It was Plazo.

Hearing his voice after so long, Courtney couldn't hold back her tears.

"Where...where have you been? I...I been—."

"It's a long story, baby."

"I got time! You don't know what I've been through not hearing your voice. It's been hard! So, if you could call me, and didn't...I don't know what to say."

Plazo explained his situation.

How he was being charged for the hospital incident for destruction of property. A petty crime. And since he refused to give up Tye's name, he was having trouble going home. Luckily, he had a good lawyer, who is working overtime to get him out.

"You did all that for Lawson?"

"I did that for both of you! Not about to see his father go back for violating probation. I just couldn't do it. And I didn't want to hear you tell me all the reasons why I should. So I just made moves."

Courtney listened; this is why she loved this man.

"Now what's going on with you, bae? You've been holding up?"

She wanted to tell him about her fears and plans, but she held back. Besides, there was nothing he could do inside. Instead, they talked about everything and nothing, savoring the conversation and the sound of each other's voice.

It was better that way.

Especially if it would be the last time she ever talked to him if things didn't go in her favor.

CHAPTER THIRTY-TWO

Courtney burst into her studio, tears streaming down her face. Adrienne was startled by her flurry of activity. The stress and fear were in her voice as she said, "Roberto and Victor are after me again! They're after my family! Why won't they leave me the fuck alone?"

Although Courtney was stressed, Adrienne was relieved. Relieved that she hadn't been caught being a snake and relieved that she was able to stay around Courtney a little bit longer. Up to that moment, Courtney had been avoiding her like the plague. So this was different.

"Is there anything I can do to help?" Adrienne asked, fake concern evident in her tone.

Courtney, struggling to maintain her composure, explained her immediate worry. "I need to get Lawson."

"Okay. Where is he?"

"He's going to be at the hotel, but there might be eyes on it now."

Adrienne frowned. This may have been too much. But if she was going to continue to play the dutiful friend, she had to go hard. "What's wrong with you, girl! I thought I told you to stop letting him stay at hotels. It's not safe."

Courtney wiped her eyes. "I should have listened," she admitted, fighting back more tears. "But I need him here, safe. Can you get him?"

"Why me?" She wanted to hear Courtney say she considered her to be a friend. Knowing that no one picked up her son unless she trusted them.

"Because you've been my most loyal friend. After all these years. And I need you. Can you do it please?"

She smiled. "Don't worry. I'll do it. I'll make sure he lays low in the backseat. He'll be safe." She grabbed her purse and bolted out the door.

Adrienne was feeling herself.

Things were looking up for her now. Prior to Courtney coming to the studio she thought she would have to start all over. But now, it appeared not only that this was far from the truth, but that their relationship had leveled up.

Parking in front of the hotel, she looked around to make sure no one had eyes on them. Her plan was going to be, too bring Lawson back to the studio.

Once there she was sure Courtney would be indebted to her forever. But plans changed when she got to the hotel room and didn't see Lawson.

Because, when Adrienne arrived and opened the door using the key card Courtney gave her, she found Tye Gates and baby father #1 waiting. Tye's gaze was piercing, his question direct and he was sitting on the edge of the bed. "What's all this for, Adrienne? What's your intent being around my son's mother?"

Adrienne, caught off guard, stammered. "I don't know what you're talking about."

"Why the fuck are you hanging around my baby mother? Why you lying about your last name?"

"Okay, if you want the truth, here it is! I was...getting information for Joanne. Because Courtney ruined everything when she got you arrested. So I was going to make her pay. My sister wanted that. Y'all were going to have a future. And that bitch took everything from you. So in a way I was going to make her pay for you both."

"The thing is, that's not true," Tye said sharply. At that moment, Joanne Davenport emerged from the bathroom, adding to the tension.

"What are you doing, Adrienne?" Joanne demanded. "Help it makes sense."

Now Adrienne needed to take a seat. Propping up in a chair by the table, she tried desperately to catch her breath. Tears started to roll down her cheeks, her shit crumbling under the weight of her deceit.

Tye revealed the extent of her betrayal. "There's no need in you lying anymore. Do you have anything you want to say?"

Silence.

"Well, let me tell you what Courtney found out. That you've been stealing from sponsors. She learned that you've been taking credit card numbers for small businesses to shout them out on the podcast without even letting them know what was going on. Some girl named Keisha looked into it after some grassfed hotdog thing? I don't even know what the fuck she was talking about for real."

At this point, Adrienne broke down completely, her lies bare for all to see. "Why you involved?"

"Because you my ex-fiancé sister. You put me in the mix of this shit."

"So what now?"

"First let me say Courtney's giving you options. Repay the $100,000 you stole or get locked the fuck up. I'm gonna be honest, I told her she should go in hard. Especially after hearing how you scared her and my son. But, that's not how she sees it though."

For the moment, Adrienne got cocky. "Do you really wanna mess with my family?"

"I don't give a fuck to tell you the truth. But we got evidence locked away, against any retaliation from the Davenports. I'm talking about everything you did is in a safe that if something happens to us, somebody's gonna get the package. That goes for myself, my son or Courtney."

Joanne, tears in her eyes, intervened. The family's reputation, their newfound stability, and their brother's political ambitions were at stake.

"We gonna take care of this, sister."

Adrienne for the moment was relieved.

"Like always." Joanne glared. "Like that time you had to go to drug rehab because you was popping pills and was asshole naked in the middle of a street. Or that time you stole all the money from the church for drugs and we came through. Daddy is done, but he told me to tell you that this will be the last time."

Adrienne was relieved. "Thank you so much!"

"I'm not done, bitch. If we do this, you'll have to relocate overseas. Like I said nobody is bailing you out anymore. Folks are doing big business and you're creating big drama."

"Do I have a choice? About leaving?"

"Nah." She breathed deeply. "Now get out. One of daddy's men will be following you. If you're not at the airport tomorrow, there's going to be trouble."

Once Adrienne left, Joanne turned her attention to Tye, attempting to lighten the mood. "I know you're sick of us aren't you?"

He stood on his feet. "To be honest I just want shit to be chill."

"You look like you still hate me."

"I never hated you."

"Do you ever think of me? I mean, do you ever think of us?"

"No. But I know you know that already."

She took a deep breath. The conversation soon turned serious. Joanne, seeking closure, asked Tye the question that had been haunting her.

She moved closer and gave him a soft kiss. "I wrote you for months when you were first arrested. All letters returned to sender. You never loved me. My only question is are you in love with Courtney?"

Tye's response was heartfelt and honest. "Yeah. But she'll never know."

CHAPTER THIRTY-THREE

With Adrienne's betrayal exposed and her departure imminent, Courtney set her plan into motion. She needed the woman out of her way without telling her that she was on to her.

The shit worked. Tye gave her an update.

Her next plan was high risk. But it was the only way to draw out Victor and Roberto and end their threat once and for all.

The decoy was simple yet effective. Courtney would appear vulnerable and alone in her home, the windows open, seemingly unaware of the danger lurking outside.

Meanwhile, two of Yo-Yo's baby fathers were positioned strategically within the house, hidden from view but ready to act at a moment's notice. They were not alone because outside, the street was subtly lined with family members and allies, each stationed in cars, appearing nonchalant but acutely alert to any movement toward Courtney's house.

No one expected or saw them unless you were paying close attention.

As Adrienne drove towards Courtney's house, intending to confront her one last time, she caught sight of Posea parked in a black pick-up truck. His attention was laser-focused on the house, oblivious to her presence. But she saw him.

She hesitated, then backed away, lights out, while parking out of sight. From her vantage point, she noticed even more of Courtney's family members scattered discreetly around the block. All with their eyes on the house.

"You smart bitch."

Realizing that Courtney was far from vulnerable and that she was surrounded by a trap she made a quick decision.

She called Roberto, her voice urgent. "I don't know what Courtney's been doing lately to make you think she doesn't see you but be careful. Because if you're planning on hitting Courtney's house tonight, think again. The whole block is hot. It's a setup."

"Who is this?"

"Somebody who knows a lot. If you want to end up dead, then disregard my message."

"How did you get my number?"

"You called the studio one million times."

"Oh, so you that girl who kept hanging up on me. Why should we trust you?"

"I don't have to convince you to trust me. But if you want a better way of getting her, there's a camera in her studio. I'm going to text you the link to watch it online. You can see her anytime you want. And find out her real moves."

With her warning delivered, Adrienne left the scene with a smile on her face. She had played her part in the dangerous game, and now it was time to disappear.

The air was crisp on the cool night as Courtney paced in her living room. Dressed in a soft yellow nightgown that fluttered around her ankles, she moved with a deliberate restlessness between the living room and the kitchen. In her hand, a glass of something strong, the liquid swirling with each step she took.

It was all for show.

Wanting to appear even more off guard, she raised her phone to her ear, engaging in a fake conversation. Her voice was intentionally loud enough to be heard from outside. Every now and again, she peered out the window, as if anxiously expecting someone.

Then, unexpectedly, her phone rang.

The sound sliced through the quiet of the night, startling her. Her heart raced as she answered, the facade momentarily slipping. Everyone, she fucked with knew not to call her at the moment.

The games were over.

Roberto's voice, cold and mocking, came through the line. "Good job, Courtney," he sneered. "But we're not stupid enough to fall for that shit."

Courtney's grip tightened, her earlier act of vulnerability replaced by a surge of adrenaline. "I don't know what you're talking about."

"You can play that game if you want to. We just wanted to make one thing clear," he said with a chilling calmness. "You're not going to have a single day of peace. You might forget, get comfortable, but we won't. We're always going to be there, lurking in the shadows. And when we're ready, we gonna take off your fucking head."

Courtney's breath hitched in her throat. Roberto's threat hung heavy in the air, a sinister promise of unending conflict.

She ended the call, mind racing. Then her phone rang again. "H...hello."

"So you got me. But just so you know, I got you too."

Courtney glared. "What was all this shit about?"

"You know I asked myself that question. At first I thought I was doing it for my sister. Because I knew how much she wanted Tye. But after a while, I wanted the money. But I stole so much from you that I didn't even need that anymore. So it became about something else."

"What was it about whore?" She yelled.

"You were too confident. Too easily able to overcome the shit that brought you to the podcast."

"So you lie? Harass me with the comments flooding our platform? Make me think people were circling in front of the studio? Put shit on my doorstep?"

"Don't forget my other work. I had my friend hit your car on the side of the road. Even scratched your car too. It was hilarious how every time I did it, you would have to get your car repaired right about the time we paid ourselves out for the podcast."

"People died, whore! And if I never fucked with the Glam Girls, I wouldn't have a problem with Roberto and Victor."

Suddenly she could hear her crying on the other end.

Courtney wanted to hang up but she had to know.

Slowly, Adrienne said, "I remember this story my mother told me. It was about two friends who started a journey through a dense, foggy path. At first, they clung to each other. But then, one friend found a flashlight and let go of the other's hand. As she walked ahead, her path became clear and bright, but the other, without a light of her own, felt left in the shadows."

"So you just wanted me to be afraid."

Silence.

"You could've said misery loves company."

"You're gonna die, bitch," Adrienne said hanging up. "Be miserable in hell."

CHAPTER THIRTY-FOUR

Back at her studio, Courtney was hosting a podcast. Posea and Yo-Yo's Baby father #1, was also present. Ever since their last attempt on Roberto and Victor a week ago ended in vain, they never left her side. But days had passed and she was no longer afraid.

In fact, she was excited because she had plans for her future which meant starting all over. But first she had to address her fans. Her video was on, and she was showing her face, while wearing a cute, purple and gold bonnet.

"Welcome back to a very special and final, episode of *'An Ugly Girls Diary'* podcast. I'm your host, and with me today in the studio are some very brave souls who've been my rock. Guys, say hello."

Baby father, #1 grumbled in the background as his way to say hello, but he left it at that.

"Hey, everyone." Posea said, more willing to take the mic.

"That's my brother! And I love him dearly! When I tell you how he rode for me, words don't do it justice." She took a deep breath. "But today I want to talk about the journey. How this podcast started as a diary of pain and transformed into a voice of strength. It's been a wild ride. Because what began as a channel for my anger, a way to cope with betrayal, turned into something more...a voice for the unheard, a community for the lonely."

"And you've helped so many people," Posea said. "I've seen that shit with my own eyes!" Courtney had no idea he was the podcasting type, but he seemed to enjoy the mic.

She would remember it for the future.

"I hope so. But I couldn't have done it without you. The support, the love, the encouragement. It's been overwhelming." She breathed deeply. "And now, as I prepare for a reinvention, for a new chapter, I want to thank each and every one of you. My listeners, my supporters, my family. I'll always be grateful for this particular chapter. So, stay tuned. When I come back, it will be with a new podcast, a new name, a new theme, but the same old me, just a little wiser and a lot stronger."

Her brother winked. Very proud of her in that moment.

"Before we go, I want to give a special thanks to our sponsor. When you want to look cute, even at bedtime, 'Sleep Pretty with Tasha's Bee Nets'." She touched the bonnet and winked. "Well, signing off for the last time before the first time, thank you, and goodbye."

They both took off the headsets and Courtney placed the bonnet in her Louis Vuitton purse. Posea stood next to her. "You ready?"

"If you mean ready to be with my son in our new home without having to worry about bullshit? I'd say yes." She picked up her purse and they locked up the studio.

Once in the parking lot Posea said, "I'm going to take her." He told the baby father. "You go keep an eye on the boy."

"Always." They dapped and pulled off.

It took about 40 minutes, but Posea drove her to the new location in Upper Marlboro, Maryland. Although there was big money in the black community, her house was a bit different. The small home needed repair, including a broken-down shack in the back. Since she had cousins and a brother, who would do anything for her it could easily be fixed up.

When they walked into the living room, Courtney took a look at bare walls, bare floors, and emptiness. "I have a long way to go don't I?"

"It's gonna be good."

"I know. But at least I feel safe," she said looking around to see what she needed, which was literally everything. "I'll go shopping tomorrow to get this place sorted."

"Okay you freshen up, and I'll make some runs and come back in a few hours. You sure you gonna be fine?"

"I would appreciate the privacy. We've been together nonstop for days."

"And here I was thinking you loved a nigga."

"I do, that's why I'm trying to separate for a little while before I kill you."

He chuckled. "Don't get too comfortable. I'm coming back, I don't care what you say," he replied firmly.

They hugged, and he walked out the door.

Left alone, she started running a bath. The tub was on the lower level and she cleaned it several times so she felt comfortable soaking for a moment. She may not have had a lot, but she had the basics. Soap, bleach, cleaner, a towel and a washcloth.

Other than that the house was still bare, so she kept her purse with her since there was no table. Suddenly, a noise entered the silence - the sound of the front door being kicked in and wood shattering.

Panic surged through her as she recognized the intrusion.

Her eyes widened.

"Posea, is that you?"

Of course it wasn't.

He would've said something.

Naked, and without a second thought, she dashed out the bathroom, purse in hand. Running towards the back door, her heart pounding, she sprinted towards the old shack, the only place to hide.

The night had taken a dangerous turn, and she was once again in the fight for her life.

It was a bitterly cold fucking night, as Courtney Martin shivered, not just from the chill but from the realization of where she found herself. An uninviting shack she had no business being inside in the first place.

She was completely naked.

Beside her lay her large Louis Vuitton purse, its contents haphazardly scattered on the ground. The most valuable item she had was her cell phone, which, frustratingly, had no service. Equally important was her diary, her constant companion.

Something she wrote in every day.

While her teeth chattered, she berated herself for her foolishness, for getting entangled in a game she had willingly played, yet she knew anyone in her situation would have fought tooth and nail for what they believed was rightfully theirs.

But it wasn't just any fight. It was for her life's work, her sense of security.

Her fucking money.

She refused to be robbed of it again!

Not after fighting so hard.

Surveying the shack, Courtney's eyes landed on a milk crate and an old, stiff potato sack. The cold sharpened her wits. What was she going to do? Use the sack for warmth or lay it on the crate to avoid splinters piercing her skin.

She chose to put it on the crate.

Once settled, she peered through the wooden slats in front of her. The world outside was covered in darkness, save for a distant house with a lit window. She decided to stay motionless, more frozen than ever, for this standoff of her life.

By T. STYLES

Diving back into her purse, she retrieved her diary.

Regret flickered through her heart because a knife or even the retractable bat she owned would have been more useful in this situation. Yet she knew dwelling on 'what ifs' wouldn't help. She needed a clear mind.

Maybe her diary could provide clarity.

Opening the flap to the first dated entry six months ago.

Courtney began to read....

Victor and Roberto, stepping out of the house, walked slowly towards the shack, their movements deliberate in the still night. The overgrown grass around the small structure whispered under their feet, a subtle yet eerie sound in the otherwise silent surroundings.

The cold air bit at their skin, the chill of the night seeping into their bones. The quietness was profound.

After months, they finally caught her alone. Both Roberto and Victor decided that they wouldn't kill her right away. Instead, they would have some fun with her. See how it would feel to have sex with her, before taking her life.

They made a mistake.

As they neared the shack, two figures emerged from the sides of the house, silhouetted against the dim moonlight. It was Baby father #1 and #2, their presence unexpected.

Victor and Roberto turned around to take off, only to find Posea and Tye standing behind them, effectively trapping them. All with guns aimed in their direction.

Courtney emerged from the shack then, wrapped in the coarse potato sack that did little to conceal her body. "Y'all made me work hard for this plan. Had a bitch get naked and everything. You don't think I saw that camera you put in my house? But when it comes to protecting my son and my family, I'm willing to do anything," she declared, her voice steady and unwavering. "Even faking being alone and wearing a potato sack."

Her crew closed in, and quickly disarmed Victor and Roberto, their movements practiced and efficient.

Roberto felt stupid. "This was slick. I mean, how did you know we knew this address? The camera in your studio?" Roberto asked, fear creeping into his voice.

Courtney shook her head. "No, I knew that would be too easy. To just give up the info on a camera installed by a snake," she said, a clear reference to Adrienne. "I figured y'all were too smart for that. So I did what you suggested, and pretended I let my guards down. Finally, I had Sakura write a letter to me. Left my address visible so that snake she shares a cell with would see it. Knowing Denise bonded with Bree and Jasmine due to their hate for me. And sure enough y'all would come running if they gave the info to you even though from what I hear, y'all still not together. I also made sure Denise's jaw got wired since she fucked with my friend."

"What happens now?" Roberto asked, his voice quivering with fear. Beside him, Victor who was numb.

"Y'all should have let it go." She said plainly.

"What happens now?" Roberto repeated.

Courtney pointed to the shack and took a deep breath. "You're just going to take a walk to the shack," she said. "It's cold, but it's a beautiful night to die."

"There has to be something we can do to convince you that we gonna go away."

"Nah...you killed my Yo-Yo."

The Baby fathers escorted Victor and Roberto forward. At first, they tried to fight, but it ended with both of them being struck multiple times in the face. In Yo-Yo's honor.

When Baby father #1 and #2 stepped back out, they were alone.

Courtney and her family stood in silence, facing each other. Under the moonlight.

The deed was done.

Yo-Yo was avenged.

Words were unnecessary, their actions spoke volumes. In the cold, moonlit night, they each processed what had occurred.

The silence was a testament to their bond, their unspoken understanding, and the lengths they were willing to go to protect one another.

CHAPTER THIRTY-FIVE

Dear Diary,

Is it wrong to say that I love life?

It's just that I've never been much at peace before now. So this feels like a drug.

Everything has worked out for me. And when I say everything I mean everything. I have the man of my dreams. My son is thriving. His relationships with his cousins and father is tighter than ever.

And if Lawson keeps catching that ball the way he's been doing, he'll get himself a football scholarship for sure.

Even my podcast, which I call simply "The Diary", where I read the pages of diaries, no matter positive or negative, as long as they're real, from my listeners, is a major success.

Yep, I'm good.

Courtney closed her diary.

The sound of footsteps interrupted her thoughts. She looked up to see Plazo, entering the room. She greeted him with a warm kiss. "Writing in that thing again?"

"You don't know by now that I write in my diary, no matter what?"

"Tye's here to pick up Lawson. He's asking if the cousins can tag along."

"Why don't you ask the Baby fathers? They're out back grilling," Courtney replied, a playful tone in her voice.

"What am I, a messenger?" Plazo laughed, teasingly.

Shaking her head, Courtney stood and walked through her new beautifully furnished house. The walls were adorned with pictures – snapshots of happier times, family portraits, and new memories they were creating. On the living room table and in the kitchen, fresh cut flowers added a splash of color and life, their fragrance subtly perfuming the air. Her new house, where only a few people knew where she lived, was a sanctuary and provided her with peace.

Outside, she relayed the message to the Baby fathers, who were tending to the grill. They readily agreed to let their sons join as Tye did good with the boys.

Tye on the other hand, was in the living room, engaged in a playful tussle with Lawson, their laughter filling the space. It was a heartwarming scene, a father and son bonding, making up for lost time.

Suddenly their moment was interrupted by the arrival of a delivery truck. Tye separated from his son, signed for a package, and brought it inside.

"They said it's a go," Courtney told Tye entering into the living room.

Lawson, and his cousins cheered. She didn't always know what Tye did with the boys, but they loved spending time with him.

"Okay we'll grab something to eat and then probably have a video game tournament. I always whip up on them anyway." He winked. "But this just came for you. They dropped it off."

Courtney, curious, took the package from him. When she broke the seal, inside was a leather-bound diary, its cover elegant yet ominous. Rusted, black leather, with a pair of high heel shoes, and a knife embossed in the middle in what look like old gold.

"What's that?" Lawson said moving in.

The Baby fathers and Plazo walked in her direction too.

As she opened the flap, the insidious nature of the gift became apparent – words written in blood greeted her, sending a shiver down her spine.

Everyone gathered around, the atmosphere turning heavy. The message in the diary was a stark reminder that, despite their victories, their struggles were far from over.

"Not again," Tye whispered.

Within These Pages, Meet Your Fate

It appeared that the war was over, but this wasn't the end of their story. The new diary, with its blood-written warning, was a clear message that their fight was ongoing, that peace would always be a hard-fought battle for Courtney and her loved ones.

Plazo walked up to her and looked into her eyes, "Bae, all you gotta do is close the cover. And it'll be like nothing ever happened."

She took a deep breath.

By T. STYLES

The Cartel Publications Order Form

www.thecartelpublications.com

Inmates **ONLY** receive novels for $12.00 per book **PLUS** shipping fee **PER BOOK.**

(Mail Order **MUST** come from inmate directly to receive discount)

Shyt List 1	_____	$15.00
Shyt List 2	_____	$15.00
Shyt List 3	_____	$15.00
Shyt List 4	_____	$15.00
Shyt List 5	_____	$15.00
Shyt List 6	_____	$15.00
Pitbulls In A Skirt	_____	$15.00
Pitbulls In A Skirt 2	_____	$15.00
Pitbulls In A Skirt 3	_____	$15.00
Pitbulls In A Skirt 4	_____	$15.00
Pitbulls In A Skirt 5	_____	$15.00
Victoria's Secret	_____	$15.00
Poison 1	_____	$15.00
Poison 2	_____	$15.00
Hell Razor Honeys	_____	$15.00
Hell Razor Honeys 2	_____	$15.00
A Hustler's Son	_____	$15.00
A Hustler's Son 2	_____	$15.00
Black and Ugly	_____	$15.00
Black and Ugly As Ever	_____	$15.00
Ms Wayne & The Queens of DC **(LGBTQ+)**	_____	$15.00
Black And The Ugliest	_____	$15.00
Year Of The Crackmom	_____	$15.00
Deadheads	_____	$15.00
The Face That Launched A Thousand Bullets	_____	$15.00
The Unusual Suspects	_____	$15.00
Paid In Blood	_____	$15.00
Raunchy	_____	$15.00
Raunchy 2	_____	$15.00
Raunchy 3	_____	$15.00
Mad Maxxx (4th Book Raunchy Series)	_____	$15.00
Quita's Dayscare Center	_____	$15.00
Quita's Dayscare Center 2	_____	$15.00
Pretty Kings	_____	$15.00
Pretty Kings 2	_____	$15.00
Pretty Kings 3	_____	$15.00
Pretty Kings 4	_____	$15.00

250   By **T. STYLES**

Silence Of The Nine	_____	$15.00
Silence Of The Nine 2	_____	$15.00
Silence Of The Nine 3	_____	$15.00
Prison Throne	_____	$15.00
Drunk & Hot Girls	_____	$15.00
Hersband Material **(LGBTQ+)**	_____	$15.00
The End: How To Write A _____		$15.00
Bestselling Novel In 30 Days (Non-Fiction Guide)		
Upscale Kittens	_____	$15.00
Wake & Bake Boys	_____	$15.00
Young & Dumb	_____	$15.00
Young & Dumb 2: Vyce's Getback	_____	$15.00
Tranny 911 **(LGBTQ+)**	_____	$15.00
Tranny 911: Dixie's Rise **(LGBTQ+)**	_____	$15.00
First Comes Love, Then Comes Murder	_____	$15.00
Luxury Tax	_____	$15.00
The Lying King	_____	$15.00
Crazy Kind Of Love	_____	$15.00
Goon	_____	$15.00
And They Call Me God	_____	$15.00
The Ungrateful Bastards	_____	$15.00
Lipstick Dom **(LGBTQ+)**	_____	$15.00
A School of Dolls **(LGBTQ+))**	_____	$15.00
Hoetic Justice	_____	$15.00
KALI: Raunchy Relived	_____	$15.00
(5th Book in Raunchy Series)		
Skeezers	_____	$15.00
Skeezers 2	_____	$15.00
You Kissed Me, Now I Own You	_____	$15.00
Nefarious	_____	$15.00
Redbone 3: The Rise of The Fold	_____	$15.00
The Fold (4th Redbone Book)	_____	$15.00
Clown Niggas	_____	$15.00
The One You Shouldn't Trust	_____	$15.00
The WHORE The Wind		
Blew My Way	_____	$15.00
She Brings The Worst Kind	_____	$15.00
The House That Crack Built	_____	$15.00
The House That Crack Built 2	_____	15.00
The House That Crack Built 3	_____	$15.00
The House That Crack Built 4	_____	$15.00
Level Up **(LGBTQ+)**	_____	$15.00
Villains: It's Savage Season	_____	$15.00
Gay For My Bae **(LGBTQ+)**	_____	$15.00
War	_____	$15.00
War 2: All Hell Breaks Loose	_____	$15.00
War 3: The Land Of The Lou's	_____	$15.00
War 4: Skull Island	_____	$15.00
War 5: Karma	_____	$15.00
War 6: Envy	_____	$15.00
War 7: Pink Cotton	_____	$15.00
Madjesty vs. Jayden (Novella)	_____	$8.99
You Left Me No Choice	_____	$15.00
Truce – A War Saga (War 8)	_____	$15.00
Ask The Streets For Mercy	_____	$15.00
Truce 2 (War 9)	_____	$15.00

An Ace and Walid Very, Very Bad Christmas (War 10) _____ $15.00
Truce 3 – The Sins of The Fathers (War 11) _____ $15.00
Truce 4: The Finale (War 12) _____ $15.00
Treason   _____ $20.00
Treason 2   _____ $20.00
Hersband Material 2 **(LGBTQ+)** _____ $15.00
The Gods Of Everything Else (War 13) _____ $15.00

The Gods Of Everything Else 2 (War 14) _____ $15.00
Treason 3   _____ $15.99
An Ugly Girl's Diary   _____ $15.99
The Gods Of Everything Else 3 (War 15) _____ $15.99
An Ugly Girl's Diary 2   _____ $19.99
King Dom **(LGBTQ+)**   _____ $19.99
The Gods Of Everything Else 4 (War 16) _____ $19.99
Raunchy: The Monsters Who Raised Harmony _____ $19.99
An Ugly Girl's Diary 3   _____ $19.99

(**Redbone 1 & 2** are **NOT** Cartel Publications novels and If **ordered** the cost is **FULL** price
of $16.00 **each plus shipping. No Exceptions.**)

Please add **$7.00** for shipping and handling fees for up to **(2) BOOKS PER ORDER**.
(INMATES INCLUDED) (See next page for details)

The Cartel Publications * P.O. BOX 486 OWINGS MILLS MD 21117

Name: _____

Address: _____

City/State: _____

Contact/Email: _____

Please allow 10-15 BUSINESS days Before shipping.

***PLEASE NOTE DUE TO **COVID-19** SOME ORDERS MAY TAKE UP TO **3 WEEKS OR LONGER**
BEFORE THEY SHIP***

The Cartel Publications is **NOT** responsible for **Prison Orders** rejected!

NO RETURNS and NO REFUNDS
NO PERSONAL CHECKS ACCEPTED
STAMPS NO LONGER ACCEPTED

By T. STYLES

Printed in the USA
CPSIA information can be obtained
at www.ICGtesting.com
LVHW020806270224
772868LV00013B/251

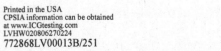